This is the work of a screenplay I wrote and decided to publish so all audiences would be able to enjoy it. A special thanks to the handful of people that read my script to help me edit and improve the story.

The Marigold List

by

B. A. Steele

EXT. MARIE'S HOUSE - NIGHT

COP 1 and COP 2 pound on the front door of a small
house with haste.

                    COP 1
          Open the door, we just want to
          talk!

                    COP 2
          You have so much to live for,
          don't do this!

INT. MARIE'S BEDROOM - NIGHT

MARIE (36) is frail and pale, she sits on the edge of her
bed. She has the barrel of a .40 silver S&W revolver held
under her chin. Marie rocks back and forth with frantic
eyes and cries.

                    MARIE
              (whispers)
          I can't. I can't.

She rocks until she looks up from the ground like she sees
someone.

                    MARIE (CONT'D)
          I have to.

She nods. Marie takes her last deep breath and pulls the
trigger.

EXT. MARIE'S HOUSE - NIGHT

The cops are frozen. It's too late for them to save her,
their heads drop.

The cops barge through her door and run inside.

INT. MARIE'S BEDROOM - NIGHT

Marie lies lifeless on her bed with blood splattered
everywhere. The cops cringe at the mess. On her bed lies a
black Glock 9mm with its empty casing.

Cop 1 observes the gun and then the wound in her head.

                    COP 1
          Hmm...

Cop 1 continues with his process.

INT. DOCTOR'S OFFICE - DAY

EMILY JOHNSON (26, African American/Caucasian) is beautiful
and has tan skin that glows, but she doesn't feel the same
as she looks.

She sits with DOCTOR BURKHART,(40) a woman with so much
experience in this field she's almost tired of it.

                    DOCTOR BURKHART
          You need more than just a higher
          dose or new pills. Since you're
          still having symptoms, I suggest
          that you find a help group.

                    EMILY
          You mean like talk to friends
          more?

                    DOCTOR BURKHART
          No, like a support group with
          other people that have depression,
          not just friends. Group therapy
          where a professional leads the
          discussion.

                    EMILY
          I don't feel comfortable with
          that, I'd rather just do what
          we've been doing.

The doctor becomes stern when Emily doubts her professional
opinion.

                    DOCTOR BURKHART
          Emily, these pills aren't good for
          prolonged use and you've been on
          them for almost ten years.

                    EMILY
          I know but-

                    DOCTOR BURKHART
          I'll give you another months
          prescription while you find a
          support group of your choice.

                    EMILY
          Okay but wait, can we-

                    DOCTOR BURKHART
          Make an appointment with me in
          three months to tell me if they're
          helping or not.

Emily stares with a blank expression.

Doctor Burkhart writes a prescription on a slip of paper and hands it to Emily. Emily gently takes the paper. Doctor Burkhart walks to the door and waits for Emily to get up and leave first.

Emily gets the hint and walks out with her head down. The doctor shuts the door behind them.

EXT. WILLIAM & SON CAR INSURANCE PARKING LOT - DAY

Emily wipes away heavy tears in her car. She puts makeup over her red face.

INT. WILLIAM & SON CAR INSURANCE, EMILY'S CUBICLE - DAY

Emily sits in her small cubicle and puts a headset on to take on the customer service role. Her coworker, REBECCA, (30, Caucasian, very brittle) can't help but wonder about her business all the time.

                    REBECCA
          Hey Emily, how'd the doctor's
          appointment go?

Emily prepares for the interview with her coworker and takes a deep breath in and pulls her headset off.

                    EMILY
          Fine, thanks for asking.

                    REBECCA
          So, how is it?

Emily rolls her eyes. She never makes eye contact with Rebecca.

                    EMILY
          I would imagine *it* is going how
          your divorce is.

                    REBECCA
          I don't think my divorce is that
          bad, I didn't try to kill myself.

Emily's work phone starts to ring.

                    EMILY
          Look, I gotta take this.

Emily puts her headset on and clicks a button on it. She talks in a very friendly customer service voice.

                    EMILY (CONT'D)
          Hello, William and Son Car
          Insurance, how may I help you
          today?

INT. CLAIRE'S APARTMENT - DAY

Emily's friend, CLAIRE, Caucasian, 24, and a little stout
looks at different outfits on her bed and holding them out
in front of her while on the phone.

                    CLAIRE
          You don't need to use that fake-
          ass voice on me, it's Claire.

INTERCUT with Emily's cubicle:

Emily goes back to her normal voice with that hint of
hopelessness in it.

                    EMILY
          Oh hey, what's up?

                    CLAIRE
          I tried texting you!

                    EMILY
          Yeah, I turned my phone off before
          I came into work.

                    CLAIRE
          Yea, I figured. So Myah wants to
          go to Club Forty-One for her
          birthday instead.

                    EMILY
          Okay. I'll meet you guys there at
          nine.

                    CLAIRE
          But wait! I'm getting ready right
          now-

Emily looks at the small decorative clock on her desk. She
shakes her head because it is only one in the afternoon.

                    CLAIRE (CONT'D)
          I think it's down to my red,
          strapless dress and gold, sequined
          dress.

                         EMILY
          I'm going to say gold and then
          you're going to want to wear the
          red...

                         CLAIRE
          Yeah, maybe I should wear my
          silver dress with the
          flower...okay, I'll see you later
          tonight, byes.

INT. WILLIAM & SON'S CAR INSURANCE, EMILY'S CUBICLE - DAY

The phone call with Claire ends but another call begins.
She's back to her happy voice.

                         EMILY
          Hello, William and Son Car
          Insurance, how can I help you?

An ANGRY FEMALE is on the other end of the phone. She yells
so loud and quickly it is incomprehensible. Emily keeps her
sweet voice but this damages her.

                         EMILY (CONT'D)
          Ma'am, please. I would love to
          help but I need you to calm down
          and tell me the problem.

The Angry Female is heard through the phone.

                         ANGRY FEMALE
          I've been on the phone three
          different times today with you
          assholes and you still haven't
          been able to help!

Rebecca peeks around Emily's cubicle.

                         REBECCA
          I just got done talking to her,
          she got in an accident that was
          her fault and she's just mad her
          rate is going up.

Frustrated and annoyed; Emily's head goes in her hands.

INT. CLUB 41 - NIGHT

Emily is in a tight blue dress and has a gold clutch bag.

She searches the club and finds her friends. Claire stands
in the red dress she debated about earlier. MYAH (26,

Puerto Rican) with an average build, is wearing a birthday tiara that says 26.

ALICIA, (28, African American) is the oldest and most mature of the friend group.

When Emily reaches her friends, they all joyously stand up and jump around. They greet each other as if they haven't seen each other in like, ten years.

> MYAH
> Emily!

Emily's mood and personality switch, she suddenly looks ecstatic to be here.

> EMILY
> Myah! Happy Birthday!

Emily hugs Myah then goes for Claire.

> CLAIRE
> Hey babes, how's it goin'?

> EMILY
> Hey doll, I see you went with the
> red dress.

> CLAIRE
> Only because it looks so good!

Alicia reaches to hug Emily.

> ALICIA
> Hey girl! How was your mother's?

> EMILY
> It was fine. Just dinner with a
> regular crazy person. She knew it
> was Myah's birthday so she didn't
> pull one of her guilt trips to try
> and make me stay longer.

> ALICIA
> That's good. Get Myah anything?

> EMILY
> I'm going to buy her a bottle and
> that's my gift.

> ALICIA
> (laughing)
> Yeah, my presence is her present.

The two laugh at each other.

INT. CLUB 41 - NIGHT

The four girls sit in a booth. Emily pours them all shots
from a bottle of vodka. They cheers to life and head to the
dance floor.

Alicia and Emily dance by each other and don't let any
strange men dance by them while Myah and Claire do the
opposite.

The girls take more shots together. Emily pours herself
another one after her friends turn around.

However, their fun is cut short when Myah tries to catch
her balance on Emily but falls on the floor.

INT. CLUB 41 BATHROOM - NIGHT

Myah pukes in the toilet while Emily holds her hair.

                    CLAIRE
          Awe, Myah, I feel so bad. I know
          this wasn't how you planned to be
          on your knees tonight.

Emily looks back at Claire and laughs, Alicia slaps
Claire's arm.

                    MYAH
          That would be funny if I didn't
          feel like I was going to pass out.

                    EMILY
          Did you just drink too much or did
          you eat something bad before this?

                    MYAH
          I...Uh.

Myah drops to the ground and is out cold.

                    EMILY
          Shit. I think we should call an
          ambulance.

Claire panics a little but doesn't freak out since Emily
and Alicia are calm.

                    ALICIA
          Drag her out here so she's away
          from the disgusting-ass toilet and
          keep her on her side. I'ma call
          nine-one-one.

INT. HOSPITAL EMERGENCY ROOM - NIGHT

The three girls surround Myah in their club outfits by her
hospital bed. She's awake but looks fatigued and is too
weak to talk. A DOCTOR (Female, 35) moves the curtains
over.

                    DOCTOR
          Myah Rodriguez?

                    EMILY
          Yep, that's her.

                    DOCTOR
          Alicia? You're here on your night
          off I see.

                    ALICIA
          I know, I can't get away from this
          place. How's Myah?

Emily gives Alicia a smiley smirk and they share a glare.

                    DOCTOR
          Well, I think Myah here was
          slipped a date rape drug,
          flunitrazepam.

The three girls gasp in shock.

                    ALICIA
          Think?

                    DOCTOR
          It's Ecstasy, she could have
          willingly taken it also. But if
          you guys were with her and didn't
          witness it, it was probably
          slipped right into her drink.

                    EMILY
          Is she going to be okay?

                    DOCTOR
          Oh yes. But we're going to keep
          her here until it's out of her
          system.

INT. HOSPITAL WAITING ROOM - NIGHT

The three sit and wait in chairs too close to each other
while one other STRANGER sits across the room, bored. Their
chairs face away from everything in the room.

                    CLAIRE
          Are you guys going to share an
          Uber with me or are you staying
          until Myah is discharged?

                    ALICIA
          I'ma have Shawn pick me up now, he
          can take us all home.

                    EMILY
               (smirking, laughing)
          So is that the bitch doctor you're
          always talking about?

                    ALICIA
          Bitch, yes! She talks down to all
          of us nurses like, she's just mad
          she's old.

Emily laughs.

                    ALICIA (CONT'D)
          Speaking of bitchy doctors, how'd
          your doctor's go?

                    EMILY
          Fine. My doctor wants me to go to
          a support group but I think it's
          pretty stupid. So I'm probably not
          going to.

                    ALICIA
          Yeah, well, whatever you gotta do.

Emily hesitates before she confides.

                    EMILY
          See, like I tried telling you guys
          before, even when I was at the
          club, that feeling was just taking
          over. Which is why I don't see how
          a group will change anything
          because it's a feeling I can't
          control.

                    CLAIRE
          Well, you looked pretty happy! You
          weren't having fun?

                    EMILY
          Well, yeah. Of course. It's just
          an overwhelming emotion in my head
          I can't get rid of, you know?

Alicia and Claire don't respond. Emily is a little
embarrassed.

> EMILY (CONT'D)
> Anyway. That's how the doctor
> went. Sorry. I just thought I'd
> fill you guys in some and try to
> talk about it like everyone
> suggests...

Alicia nods at Emily for reassurance and Claire keeps eye
contact with her. They don't say anything. Emily tries to
leave in an attempt to avoid the awkwardness.

> EMILY (CONT'D)
> I'm going to get a drink, you guys
> want anything?

> ALICIA
> Nah, I'm good.

> CLAIRE
> No thanks, I'm not thirsty.

Emily leaves the waiting room. Claire looks behind her to
make sure Emily isn't around anymore.

INT. HOSPITAL HALLWAY - NIGHT

Emily looks left and right for a vending machine but there
aren't any around.

INT. HOSPITAL WAITING ROOM - NIGHT

Claire and Alicia start their gossip about Emily.

> CLAIRE
> I really hate how she tries to
> drag her mood down around us.

> ALICIA
> Yeah. I know she's legit, I get
> depressed patients all the time,
> but I don't think Emily tries hard
> enough to help herself like I know
> others do.

Emily starts to approach Claire and Alicia from behind but
stops when she hears her name.

                    CLAIRE
          Like, seriously Emily? One of your
          best friends is in the hospital
          right now because someone tried to
          drug her and she's making this
          about her.

                    ALICIA
          I know like, right now isn't the
          time. We're all still a little
          drunk and there is a bigger issue
          at hand. I just asked about her
          doctor's to be nice.

                    CLAIRE
          She longs for everyone to care for
          her so bad like we don't have our
          own problems, you know? She needs
          a man.

                    ALICIA
          No, she needs to learn to like
          herself first.

Emily tries to fight her tears but can't. She slowly walks
back and out of the waiting room without her friends aware
of her absence.

INT. HOSPITAL HALLWAY - NIGHT

Emily tries to calm herself down. She makes her eyes
observe the flyers on the bulletin board next to her. Many
of them are for case studies and some of them are for help
groups.

All have a small red mark that indicates they were approved
to be on that board except one, which catches her
attention.

The unmarked flyer says: *I am here and when you are ready,
we will all be here. A help group for people who need to
talk to someone of the same. Tuesdays and Thursdays 8 pm at
Marigold Church.*

Emily wipes her tears away. She grabs the flyer.

INT. UBER CAR - NIGHT

Emily rides alone in her Uber. She fights tears.

INT. EMILY'S KITCHEN - NIGHT

Emily breaks down. She lets out everything she's held back.
She rips her shoes off and she fights to calm herself down.
Emily pulls a knife from the kitchen drawer, she presses
the knife against her wrist but stops herself.

She has heavy, constant tears. Emily lifts up her dress and
exposes her underwear and old scars from cutting herself on
her ribs, sides, and hips. She starts to cut against her
sides. Emily screams in pain.

Emily throws her knife and cries while she bleeds slowly.

                    EMILY
              (crying, whispering)
          Fuck. I deserve this.

Her cat, PAUL, rubs against her legs to greet her. Emily
calms down.

INT. EMILY'S BEDROOM - DAY

Emily's alarm strikes 7:00 a.m. She was awake before the
alarm went off but she stares at the ceiling and listens to
the annoying alarm blare.

Emily rolls out of bed in a baggy T-shirt and shorts. She
has a water bottle and a bottle of Zoloft on her
nightstand, she takes a dose.

Her cat jumps on her bed and she pets him. She still has a
blank, unmotivated stare. She finally turns the alarm off.

EXT. EMILY'S APARTMENT BUILDING - DAY

Emily walks out of her six-story apartment in business
casual clothing.

A man in business professional clothes, JOHN ACE (34,
Caucasian) who is handsome but he wouldn't know it since
he's such a shy gentleman, walks into the building. John
holds the door open for Emily as she walks out.

                    EMILY
          Thank you.

INT. WILLIAM & SON CAR INSURANCE - DAY

Emily is in her cubicle, she talks with a customer and
does paperwork.

                    EMILY
          Okay sir, thank you for calling
          William and Son's, have a nice
          day.

Emily writes out her customer report while her boss, DAVID
(30) comes over. David really lets the idea of "boss" get
to his head; his suits are always a little too short
because he doesn't know how they are supposed to fit.

                    DAVID
          How's it going, Emily? Since you
          didn't do this Monday, I need you
          to get on this accident report
          today.

                    EMILY
          Oh, that's because I've never done
          an accident report.

                    DAVID
          Ah. Okay. Stop by my desk after
          your shift, we will go over it.

David drops the file on her desk and pats her shoulder
before he leaves, Emily rolls her eyes.

INT. WILLIAM & SON CAR INSURANCE - DAY

Emily stands while she fixes folders on her desk and puts
her phone in her purse. She tries to escape past David's
room but he catches her. He calls for her from his desk.

                    DAVID
          Emily! Did you forget?

                    EMILY
          Oops! Yeah, good thing you
          reminded me. Almost. Forgot.

INT. DAVID'S OFFICE - DAY

David motions for Emily to sit while he rests behind his
desk. He adjusts his tight cuffs and tie.

                    DAVID
          So how come you don't know how to
          do an accident report?

                    EMILY
          Well, it's not a part of my
          department, so I was never taught.

                         DAVID
              Oh. I see. Okay.

David comes out from behind his desk along with a random
folder he finds. He comes by Emily's side and bends down
and puts the folder into her hands to open it. He rests his
hand on her shoulder as he talks.

                         DAVID (CONT'D)
              Well, it's very simple, see? Just
              call them and the other people
              involved to ask what they saw to
              hear their statement and point of
              view from the accident.

Emily stands up to elude how uncomfortable David makes her.
She safely makes it to the water cooler in his office.

                         DAVID (CONT'D)
              Why didn't you tell me you were
              thirsty, I could have gotten you a
              drink while I was up.

                         EMILY
              Umm, yeah. It's just easier, I
              have to hurry up here anyway
              because I need to get home to
              Paul.

                         DAVID
              Paul?

                         EMILY
                   (clears throat after
                   choking on some water)
              My-my cat.

                         DAVID
              Oh. Well, we can continue this
              tomorrow or tonight even?

                         EMILY
              Yeah, tomorrow seems fine. I come
              in at eight tomorrow, so I'll see
              you then.

                         DAVID
              Emily, you can't just leave in the
              middle of a meeting.

David scoffs as if Emily doesn't know he holds the power of
her job.

> EMILY
> Sorry, I thought you were implying
> we just finish this later. But,
> I'm pretty aware of what I have to
> do now.

> DAVID
> No, we will go over the rest
> tomorrow then, after your shift.

> EMILY
> Okay, thank you. I'll see you
> tomorrow.

Emily throws her half-full cup into the trash can and makes her way out of the office.

INT. EMILY'S APARTMENT - NIGHT

The TV sits as background noise while she bites her nails and looks at the Marigold Help Group flyer.

Emily throws on a jacket and a baseball hat and pulls it lower to cover her face.

INT. MARIGOLD CHURCH - NIGHT

Emily checks her watch, it is 7:50 pm. She enters the church with a large room and a circle of chairs.

She looks lost in the sea of people. There is chatter all around the room. Emily leaves the church.

EXT. MARIGOLD CHURCH - NIGHT

Emily walks fast to her car when she hears a man, ABE KENNEDY (37, Caucasian), yell outside the church.

> ABE
> Hey!...Hey!

Emily continues to walk.

> ABE (CONT'D)
> Ma'am, wait up!

Abe jogs to her car. He has a lot of muscle but isn't burly, and has a short, full beard on him. He's wearing a red Hawaiian shirt and jeans.

                  ABE (CONT'D)
Hey! Where are you going? Party is
inside.

                  EMILY
Sorry. Hi. I just don't want to do
this anymore.

                  ABE
Wait. It's okay. It's not that
bad, you should come inside. We
would all love to have you. You
would fit in great here!

Abe's warm smile makes Emily relax.

                  ABE (CONT'D)
My name is Abe. What is your name?

                  EMILY
Emily.

                  ABE
Hey, Emily. It would be real nice
if you came back in but I
understand if you want to leave.
You can come back Thursday, next
Tuesday, next month, or heck, come
back in an hour if you want. But,
I understand, it can be real
overwhelming, but you can just sit
and watch.

Emily smiles but doesn't know what to say back.

                  ABE (CONT'D)
Anyway, I'll leave you alone so
you can decide. Whatever makes you
happy. That's what's important.

Abe smiles and nods at Emily then walks back into the
church.

INT. MARIGOLD CHURCH - NIGHT

Emily enters the church. Eight other people fill the room.
Abe sees the decision Emily has made and nods at her.

                  ABE
All right, everyone. Startin' in
five minutes.

ROB (17) in a wheelchair comes over to greet Emily.

                    ROB
Hi, I'm Rob.

                    EMILY
Hello, Rob. I'm Emily. Nice to
meet you.

                    ROB
Yeah, you too. Hope you have a
good time tonight. I know this
place has helped me a lot.

                    EMILY
How long have you been coming
here?

                    ROB
About four months now.

                    EMILY
Well, that's good. I'm glad this
is working out for you. How old
are you if you don't mind me
asking?

                    ROB
I'm seventeen. I know. I look too
young to be in a wheelchair and be
clinically depressed.

Rob laughs at himself.

                    EMILY
No! That's not really it. I mean I
was around that age too.

                    ROB
Really? You were in a wheelchair
too?

                    EMILY
              (nervous from possibly
               insulting Rob)
No! I mean--

                    ROB
              (laughing)
Ha! I know I'm just messing with
you.

                    EMILY
              (laughing too)
Oh my God. You have a weird sense
of humor, Rob.

                    ROB
          Yeah, I need to have it.

WHITNEY (50, Caucasian) over tans and is very in shape for
her age, walks into their conversation.

                  WHITNEY
          Hi, Rob! Hi there, I'm Whitney.

                  EMILY
          Hello Whitney, I'm Emily.

Abe takes a seat in the circle of chairs.

                  WHITNEY
          I'm glad you are able to make it
          here tonight, let me know if you
          need anything, we can talk later!

Whitney hurries to a seat next to Abe. Then everyone else
grabs a seat.

                  ABE
          Good-evenin', everyone. How was
          everybody's weekend?

Everyone talks over each other about their weekend.

                  ABE (CONT'D)
          So before we start, we have a new
          addition to our group.

The people look directly at Emily knowing who the intruder
is.

                  ABE (CONT'D)
          Would you like to introduce
          yourself or just sit back?

                  EMILY
          I'm fine just watching. Thanks.

                  ABE
          Perfect. Let's get started. Like
          normal, I'll start with myself
          when we have a newcomer.

The front door of the church slams closed. John, the same
man from Emily's apartment that held the door, walks in the
room. He's in jeans, a light jacket, and also has a
baseball hat on.

Everyone is reading how nervous John is just by the way he
walks. He fills the last empty seat.

                    ABE (CONT'D)
          Hey there! Have a seat. Two new
          guests in one night, what a
          surprise. Good idea with spreading
          flyers, Whitney, they must be
          workin'.

John sits far from Emily.

                    ABE (CONT'D)
          Would you like to introduce
          yourself?

                    JOHN
               (quiet, anxious)
          Hi. I'm John. I'm new. Obviously.

                    ABE
          Thanks for doing that John, that's
          real brave of you. Would you like
          to continue?

                    JOHN
          Uh, no. Not really.
               (anxious laugh)

Abe's friendliness is surprising for John because Abe is so
nice yet masculine.

                    ABE
          No problem. We were just about to
          begin. My name is Abe. I'm here
          because, after four tours, I saw a
          lot of things that changed me. But
          that's not what is important,
          what's important is how I manage
          myself and I do that with you
          guys. All of you guys really help
          me cope knowing that I'm not
          alone. So just know that's why
          you're here, we may have different
          stories but we all feel the same
          and we're all here to help each
          other.

Abe nods to everyone and is smiling wide.

                    ABE (CONT'D)
          Why don't we go around real quick
          and let Emily and John know a bit
          about our story and the benefit of
          the help group? Erin, I know you
          said something about it last week,
          would you like to go now?

ERIN (40) has short blonde hair and has a little bit of weight on her. She sits on the right of Abe.

                    ERIN
          Of course, Abe. Hi. I'm Erin. Most
          of you know already that I've had
          clinical depression for the past
          year. I lost my child because of
          cancer and as a result of the
          stress, my husband and I split.

Erin finds it hard to talk, she tries to hold back her tears.

                    ABE
          Erin, don't forget what we worked
          on. It's okay.

Emily turns her head out of some confusion for cutting Erin's sad story off so suddenly.

                    ERIN
          Yes, you're right. Thank you.

Abe rubs Erin's back to comfort her.

                    ABE
          What I notice helps us all is
          setting goals and actually trying
          to reach them. With everyone here,
          my goal is to help improve your
          lives in all areas.

Rob raises his hand.

                    ABE (CONT'D)
          Erin, is it okay if Rob talks? He
          wants to say something.

Erin wipes a tear and nods "yes".

                    ROB
              (to Erin)
          Thanks.
              (to everyone)
          Hola. I'm Rob. I was in a car
          accident two years ago which
          killed my mom and paralyzed me.
              (beat)
          After the accident, I could never
          really handle life anymore until I
          came here.
                    (MORE)

                    ROB (CONT'D)
It really sucks being paralyzed
and losing a family member, if you
couldn't assume that already, so
coming here makes it easier to
cope with. I've become a lot more
social and open even though my
whole life I've been shy. So, I'm
hoping this group can bring you
out of your own shell. And that's
all I wanted to share...

                    ABE
Thanks for sharing, Rob. I like
that.
        (beat)
Anyone else?

Four others raise their hands.

INT. MARIGOLD CHURCH - NIGHT

Everyone takes a short break from the circle to stretch and
get their free, shitty, coffee on a stretched out table
with little sugar and cream packets. Abe walks over to John
and Emily at the table.

                    ABE
How is it going, you two? Did you
like getting to know everyone so
far?

                    EMILY
Yeah, I really like hearing other
people's backgrounds. But,
honestly, I don't think I should
be here.

                    ABE
Why would that be, Emily?

                    EMILY
Well, everyone has these intense
reasons to be here, but I've never
experienced anything like that.

                    ABE
I'm glad you're being honest with
me, Emily. But depression, it's a
disease. Some things make it
happen and sometimes it just
happens. You shouldn't compare
yourself to them since you're not
them, you know?

                    EMILY
          Yeah, I just hope I'm at the right
          kind of support group. My doctor
          recommended it and she's cutting
          off my prescriptions so that I
          have to try this.

                    ABE
          I see. Yeah, a lot of people come
          here for that and turns out, their
          doctors were right. What about
          you, John?

                    JOHN
               (caught off guard)
          Oh, I'm sorry, I'm not really
          comfortable...I don't want to talk
          about myself. As of right now, I
          mean.

                    ABE
          That's absolutely fine. Just let
          me know when you are. So we can
          help.

Abe smiles. STELLA (32) tall and slim, approaches Abe.

                    STELLA
          Abe, may I speak to you in private
          for a second?

                    ABE
          Of course, Stella.
               (to John and Emily)
          I'll see you in five when we
          re-group.

Emily and John stand there awkwardly.

                    EMILY
          You look familiar?

                    JOHN
          Yeah, I think we live in the same
          apartment building.

                    EMILY
          Oh! That makes sense. I think you
          held the door open for me today.

                    JOHN
          Yeah, sometimes it's the elevator.

They laugh at the small conversation.

                    JOHN (CONT'D)
              (laughing uncomfortably,
               scratching head)
          Yeah, I didn't think anyone I knew
          of would be here so I decided to
          come, but now I'm thinking about
          not coming back.

                    EMILY
          Why? This place seems better than
          I expected. You should totally
          stay and try it out. The people
          here are nicer than my own
          friends.

                    JOHN
          Yeah.

John closes off and shakes his head. Emily reads his body
language. John stands a little distant from her.

                    EMILY
          Anyway, I'll talk to you later.
          It's crazy that we never met or
          talked before.

INT. MARIGOLD CHURCH - NIGHT

Everyone has gathered around the circle again.

                    ABE
          Okay, everyone. Please just keep
          working on your own goals and
          making more. Meanwhile, John and
          Emily, start your Marigold list.
          Write ten goals or bucket list
          items. Short term and long term,
          and let me see them next time you
          stop by.

EXT. EMILY'S APARTMENT BUILDING - NIGHT

John holds the door open for Emily to get into the
apartment.

                    EMILY
          This is so weird. Like, we leave
          the same place just to come back
          to the same place.

                    JOHN
          Yeah, I know.

The two walk over to the elevator and John pushes the "up" button.

                    EMILY
          Are you going to go on Thursday?

                    JOHN
          Uh. I might.

                    EMILY
          I think I'm going to try it out a
          little longer. I just want to make
          sure they're not fake happy, seems
          a little too good to be true.

                    JOHN
          Well...Never mind.

                    EMILY
          What?

                    JOHN
          I just, nothing.

                    EMILY
          Just say it, now I'm curious.

The elevator dings and starts opening up.

                    JOHN
          I was just going to ask if you
          wanted to carpool but never mind.
          We don't know each other enough.
          You know, stranger danger.

Emily pushes floor two and he pushes six.

                    EMILY
          Oh right, of course. I'm
          twenty-six but I still fall back
          to that rule always.

                    JOHN
          Well good. People are fucking
          crazy.

The elevator stops on the second floor and Emily steps off.

                    EMILY
          They really are. I'll see you
          later, John. Maybe even at
          Marigold on Thursday.

                    JOHN
          Yeah, see ya. Goodnight.

John leans his back into the elevator wall and rubs his
tired face.

INT. EMILY'S APARTMENT - NIGHT

Emily unlocks her door and enters. Paul lays on the couch
watching the TV. Emily walks over to pet him.

                    EMILY
          Awe, Paul, you're so cute when you
          watch TV.

The news is on and the NEWS ANCHOR speaks.

                    NEWS ANCHOR
          Marie Campbell had committed
          suicide with a nine millimeter.
          Her family would like us to bring
          her story to light for people to
          get the help they need if they are
          not happy.

She grabs a pen and paper from the small clutter on her
table and she starts to list numbers 1-10 on it.

EXT. MARIGOLD CHURCH - NIGHT

Abe and LAUREN (30, blonde and anxious) talk outside the
church.

                    ABE
          I'm glad you decided to meet up
          with me. Why haven't you been
          coming to our meetings?

                    LAUREN
          I just don't think I need this
          anymore.

Abe's tone in voice changes. He loses his smile.

                    ABE
          Oh. I see. Well, Lauren, I don't
          think that would be a good idea
          for you.

INTERCUT between Emily's apartment and the church.

INT. EMILY'S APARTMENT - CONT'D

Emily starts with her number one goal. "Be happy". Then she
writes number two, "fall in love."

EXT. MARIGOLD CHURCH - CONT'D

Lauren is intimidated talking to Abe. She takes a step
back.

> LAUREN
> I really don't want to do this, I
> think I'm ready to be happy on my
> own and leave the help group.

> ABE
> Lauren, look how far you've come
> because of me. You can only get
> better and honestly, I'm very
> insulted that you would want to
> leave after being so loyal for
> over two years.

Lauren gets courageous and takes a step towards Abe.

> LAUREN
> I know what you're up to and I
> know what you did to Marie so I'm
> out.

INT. EMILY'S APARTMENT

Emily writes number three, "Have someone actually love me
back" and four, "Get a better job".

> NEWS ANCHOR
> Marie's family said that she was
> in a support group but left it to
> try and find herself. She had
> stopped reaching out to everyone
> and that's when her family wished
> they knew these important signs.

EXT. MARIGOLD CHURCH

Abe grins at Lauren.

> LAUREN
> I know you killed her.

> ABE
> What do you mean? You act like I'm
> the one that pulled the trigger
> for her. She killed herself! I
> can't save everyone.

INT. EMILY'S APARTMENT

Emily chews on her pen in an attempt to think of something
else. She continues. "*Five: Travel. Six: Go on a plane.
Seven: Meet my dad. Eight: Help someone else be happy*"

EXT. MARIGOLD CHURCH

Abe takes a step towards Lauren.

                    ABE
          I guess you'll be fine without us.
          But do you think you can handle
          being alone? Again?

Lauren cowers against her car but wills up some courage.

She pushes Abe away from her but he pushes her back against
her car.

                    LAUREN
          I'm not going to play your game!
          I'm not going to let you get to me
          like you did with Marie! It's not
          right what you're doing!

Lauren shoves Abe aside and gets in her car as fast as she
can. Abe smirks and backs up as Lauren drives away.

INT. EMILY'S APARTMENT

"*Nine: Do something crazy Ten: Be someone else.*" Emily
sighs at her paper and pulls out her phone.

EXT. MARIGOLD CHURCH

Abe's phone rings, his tone is back to being happy when he
answers.

                    ABE
          Hello?

INT. EMILY'S APARTMENT

Emily rises from her table while the news anchor still
speaks of Marie's death.

                    EMILY
          Hi Abe, it's Emily. I'm calling
          the number on the flyer and I hope
          it's not too late.

                        ABE
          No, of course not, you can call me
          anytime.

                        EMILY
          I just wanted to let you know that
          I think I want to keep attending
          but I had to tell you now because
          I know in the morning how
          unmotivated I will be and I don't
          want that to affect this.

                        ABE
          Yeah, of course, I completely
          understand. I'll be there to help
          you keep coming here. I know what
          this disease can do to people.
          Thanks for letting me help, Emily.

                        EMILY
          Thanks, Abe, I'll see you on
          Thursday.

Emily hangs up with a smile.

INT. EMILY'S APARTMENT BEDROOM - DAY

Emily is in her bed, her eyes open, unmotivated; she makes
a whaling sound towards that stupid Marigold Help Group
flyer on her nightstand next to her pills.

INT. WILLIAM & SON CAR INSURANCE - DAY

Emily gets through the door and Rebecca is already there to
greet her. Rebecca is holding a box of donuts.

                        REBECCA
          Emily! I got you something.
          Comfort food always helps me when
          I'm down about nothing.

Emily opens the box and there are no donuts inside, just a
vegetable tray. Rebecca laughs.

                        EMILY
               (annoyed)
          Ha. That's a good one, Rebecca.
          I'm sure everyone got a kick out
          of that.

Rebecca walks with Emily to her cubicle.

> REBECCA
> So did you hear that David is
> laying someone off?

> EMILY
> What? Who? Why?

> REBECCA
> Because he doesn't know what he's
> doing.

> EMILY
> He's probably just trying to pick
> up an extra paycheck.

Emily takes a seat in her cubicle. Rebecca sets down the disguised donuts on Emily's desk. Emily just glares at her because she doesn't want the fake donuts or Rebecca near her.

> REBECCA
> I heard it's Charlie. So sad. He's
> been here forever, and new
> management is pushing him out
> because he doesn't have boobs.

> EMILY
> Yeah, that sounds like something
> Dave would do.

Emily starts to turn her computer on. Rebecca still stands there and David walks by her cubicle.

> DAVID
> Emily, when you and Rebecca are
> done gossiping, can I speak to you
> in my office?

David continues to walk past them.

> REBECCA
> Uh oh. Maybe it's not Charlie.

> EMILY
> One can only hope.

Emily scoots out of her chair. Before she leaves she hands Rebecca her veggie tray.

> EMILY (CONT'D)
> And take your fake-ass donuts.

Rebecca laughs to herself for being so funny and original.

INT. WILLIAM & SON CAR INSURANCE, DAVID'S OFFICE - DAY

David sits on his desk with a file when Emily enters.

                    DAVID
          Okay, let's just get to the point
          because Rebecca isn't holding
          anything back for anyone.

                    EMILY
          Is someone getting fired?

                    DAVID
          Charlie was laid off this morning.

                    EMILY
          Why?

                    DAVID
          We just didn't need him anymore,
          he hasn't been doing much. And you
          know how to do accident reports
          now, I was thinking you could take
          his place.

                    EMILY
          Like instead of doing customer
          service?

                    DAVID
          Well, that you could do both. I'm
          having all representatives pick up
          the little extra slack.

                    EMILY
          Um, okay...Can I get a raise at
          least?
               (laughing)

                    DAVID
               (laughing back)
          Ha, ha, no. I'm just giving you a
          heads up. Thanks for the hard work
          so far though, keep it up.

David hands Emily a manila folder and points for her to
leave.

Emily returns to her cubicle and Rebecca peeks around the
corner with a carrot from her vegetable tray.

                    REBECCA
          So what'd you guys talk about?

                    EMILY
What crawled up his ass? He's
being a real douche lately. I miss
creepy Dave.

                    REBECCA
I think he has a girlfriend now.
Even though he blocked me I have
another Facebook account that I
use anyway and it looks like he
has new arm candy.

                    EMILY
Why'd he block you?

                    REBECCA
I don't know why, but I get
blocked by a lot of people.

INT. MARIGOLD CHURCH - NIGHT

Emily waits her turn to speak with Abe. She's wearing her
usual hat and jacket with her purse. Abe excuses himself
from Erin and Whitney.

                    ABE
Emily! Glad to see you back. Did
you make a list?

                    EMILY
I did!

Emily digs for the list in her purse.

                    EMILY (CONT'D)
I hope it is good enough.

                    ABE
Of course, as long as it's what
you want.

He reads the paper she hands him.

                    ABE (CONT'D)
This is great. Is it okay if we
share this with the group today?

                    EMILY
Oh, I don't know it's kind of
personal...

                    ABE
          Well, my goal is that when we
          share with them, they can help you
          accomplish these so you're not
          alone through anything.

                    EMILY
          I mean, I guess you're the expert
          here, I should probably just trust
          the system, you know?

                    ABE
          Yeah, but it's easier when you're
          comfortable. So whenever you want
          to share, just let me know and
          we'll take that step.

                    EMILY
          It's just so weird when all these
          people are on different levels
          than me. They probably already
          made a list and are done with
          them.

                    ABE
          They're working on their goals but
          everyone here is always making
          more. And all of us are helping
          each other with them.

                    EMILY
          Yeah, everyone just looks so happy
          and I'm just a little anxious that
          I won't make it to that.

                    ABE
          Make it? Like you think you might
          kill yourself soon?
               (chuckles)
          Let me see your Marigold list
          again.

Abe pulls out a pen, Emily hands him the list. He writes
down the date: "October 12"

                    ABE (CONT'D)
          October twelfth. Three months from
          now. No matter how much you want
          to off yourself, you're not doing
          it in between now and October
          twelfth.

He draws an "X" at the bottom of the paper.

                    ABE (CONT'D)
          Sign here. Make it a promise. We
          won't tell anyone what it means.

Emily smiles. She signs.

                    EMILY
               (nervous laughter)
          What if I still want to kill
          myself after the three months?

                    ABE
          Ask me that in a few months. I
          have faith in my system that you
          won't want to.

Abe smiles and winks at her.

                    ABE (CONT'D)
          So, if John shows up, would you
          like to just show your list to him
          since he's new too?

                    EMILY
          That would be nice. We actually
          live in the same apartment
          building and I think he'd be more
          comfortable with that too.

                    ABE
          Great, we can talk to him when he
          arrives.

INT. MARIGOLD CHURCH - NIGHT

Emily is getting herself some coffee and John comes up to
her.

                    JOHN
          Hey, how's it going?

                    EMILY
          Hey! Fancy meeting you here. Make
          a list?

                    JOHN
          Yep. And checked it twice.

                    EMILY
          Good. I was talking to Abe and he
          suggested that if you're not
          comfortable talking to everybody
          about what's on there, we could
          just do it together.

John doesn't give any real response.

                    EMILY (CONT'D)
          But that's because I figured Abe
          knows what he's doing and I should
          start somewhere.

                    JOHN
          Yeah. I guess.

                    EMILY
          But, you know. That's just
          something we talked about without
          you so, just a thought!

                    JOHN
          Makes sense. You're a familiar
          face, I can see what he means.

                    EMILY
          Yeah, exactly what I was thinking.

Abe walks up from behind them.

                    ABE
          You guys ready for some fun? Come
          take a seat. Nice to see you
          again, John.

John and Abe shake hands.

INT. EMILY'S APARTMENT DOOR - NIGHT

Emily unlocks her apartment door while John waits outside.

                    EMILY
          Okay, wait there, let me make sure
          it's decently clean.

INT. EMILY'S KITCHEN - NIGHT

Emily places her purse on the counter. She scurries to the
kitchen and throws two cups in the dishwasher and throws a
rag in the sink.

INT. EMILY'S DINING/LIVING ROOM - NIGHT

She straightens papers on her dining room table and fixes a
few couch cushions; nothing in her house is too out of
order.

INT. EMILY'S APARTMENT DOOR - NIGHT

Emily picks up Paul and opens the door.

> EMILY
> You're not allergic to cats, are
> you?

> JOHN
> No.

John pats the cat's head.

> EMILY
> Alright then, let's get started!

INT. EMILY'S LIVING ROOM - NIGHT

Emily sits on her couch and sets Paul down. She takes off
her jacket and hat then reaches for her list in her pocket.

John slowly walks towards the couch. Emily sets her phone
on the living room table.

John notices the potted tree in the corner and the
decorative plant on the end table.

> JOHN
> Nice place you have here. Lots of
> plants and stuff.

John relaxes on the end of her couch. Emily faces him and
sits cross-legged.

> EMILY
> Thanks. Hope it's not too
> disorganized or sloppy looking.
> Want any water?

> JOHN
> A lot better than my place. And no
> thanks.

> EMILY
> So, what's on John's list?

> JOHN
> Nothing too special, I don't
> think.

They exchange lists.

> JOHN (CONT'D)
> I didn't get all the way to ten.

                    EMILY
          Yeah, the numbering only one
          through five gave it away.

She ponders at his list.

                    EMILY (CONT'D)
          Hmm, open up, get a dog, remarry,
          show more expression, and move
          out...Like out of here? Do you
          live with someone else?

                    JOHN
          No.

Emily waits for John to speak more but he doesn't.

                    EMILY
               (nervous laughter)
          Well c'mon, what is it? Open up!

                    JOHN
          I just had to move in here after
          my divorce and I've already been
          here for a year.

                    EMILY
          So you like the married life?

                    JOHN
          I just feel like getting married
          is what people my age are supposed
          to do.

                    EMILY
          Can I ask what happened?

                    JOHN
          Would you hang on? I didn't even
          get to your list yet! Give me a
          second.

                    EMILY
               (laughing)
          Okay, sorry.

Emily watches John closely as he reads her list. He peeks
over at her but goes back to reading. He looks back up at
her again.

                    JOHN
          Do you mind? I can't read when
          you're staring at me like that.

                    EMILY
          Everyday life must be a struggle
          for you then knowing six-year-olds
          are more capable than you.

                    JOHN
               (shaking head, smiling)
          Damn. Okay then.

John fixes the paper to read again. Emily continues to
stare and a few seconds later he puts the paper down.

                    JOHN (CONT'D)
          Alright. Neat stuff. I don't see
          how I can really help you with
          these like Abe was talking about.

                    EMILY
          It's more about the support. Like,
          be there with me while we go
          through it or do it with me, you
          know?

                    JOHN
          Oh, yeah I see now.
               (beat)
          Should we start with you or me?

                    EMILY
          Well, I think we're starting with
          yours right now.

                    JOHN
          What do you mean? Which one?

                    EMILY
          Opening up. Or expressing
          yourself. I feel like those are
          kind of the same.

                    JOHN
          Yeah, I was running out of ideas.
          It's hard to think on the spot, I
          haven't even thought of something
          else to add since.

                    EMILY
          We'll get there! So why do you
          want to open up?

John thinks about it.

                    JOHN
          I mean, I don't know.

                    EMILY
          I'm a stranger, it should be easy
          to talk to me, because guess what,
          we don't ever have to speak again
          if you don't want to.
                    (beat)
          So fire away, stranger.

                    JOHN
          Okay. I'm a Gemini.

                    EMILY
          Oh, I'm sorry.

                    JOHN
                    (laughing)
          What?

                    EMILY
                    (laughing)
          I'm just kidding! But that's a
          start.

                    JOHN
          So, I opened up some. Now let's
          pick something from your list.

                    EMILY
          I'm not sure what you could help
          with. Did I help you be happy at
          all these past twenty minutes?

                    JOHN
          It's been twenty minutes.

Emily nods her head.

                    JOHN (CONT'D)
          You can apply at my marketing
          agency since you want a better
          job, I don't know what your
          experience is.

                    EMILY
          You own a marketing agency and you
          live in this shit hole?

                    JOHN
          I told you I was divorced. It's a
          long story.

Emily's phone starts to ring on the table in front of her,
the number isn't saved.

> EMILY
> I have no idea who this could be
> especially this late...

> JOHN
> Don't pick it up then.

Emily picks her phone up from the table.

> EMILY
> I have to, I'm too curious not to
> know!
>> (in phone)
> Hello?
>> (beat)
> Oh, hi Erin? How'd you get my
> number?

Emily feeds a very confused face that makes John react with
more confusion.

> EMILY (CONT'D)
> That's totally fine and of course!
> That would be awesome. When would
> you like to go?
>> (beat)
> I'll totally invite him, he's with
> me now. Just text me.
>> (beat, sounding extra
>> happy)
> Thank you, Erin. You can call or
> text me anytime too.

Emily hangs up her phone.

> EMILY (CONT'D)
> Well, that was Erin from the help
> group. She got my number from Abe
> and wants me to help her with some
> things on her list.

> JOHN
> Oh, interesting.

Emily smiles wide. She is ecstatic about her new friend
that wants her help.

> JOHN (CONT'D)
> What are you helping her with?

                        EMILY
          She wants me to be her wing-man
          and she asked if you would like to
          come help her too because she said
          she needs all the help she can
          get.

                        JOHN
          I haven't been out in a while, not
          sure how I could help, but okay.

                        EMILY
          This is actually really fun.

John rubs his face.

                        JOHN
               (laughing uncomfortably) This
          is so fucking weird. But
          apparently, Abe knows what he's
          doing if the doctors told us to do
          this.

John raises from her couch and Emily follows.

                        EMILY
          So, Erin said she wanted to go out
          tomorrow night. I'll see if she
          wants us to just all ride
          together. Her list so I guess her
          choice.

                        JOHN
          Yeah. Put your number in my phone
          and just keep me updated.

John hands her his phone and she starts typing.

Emily finally notices the height difference with her and
John because he's so close. She smiles.

                        EMILY
          So does this mean you're like,
          going to stay in the group now?

                        JOHN
          I wouldn't say that. I'll see how
          I feel after a few more weeks.

                        EMILY
          Gee, maybe you should put
          commitment issues on that list.

                        JOHN
          I don't find those to be issues.

John takes his phone back.

                    JOHN (CONT'D)
          Thanks for inviting me over, I'll
          see ya tomorrow.

EXT. CLUB RUBY PARKING LOT - NIGHT

John and Emily lean against his white Audi A5 on the
driver's side. John wears jeans and an unbuttoned long-
sleeve over his white T-shirt. Emily is in a short, red
dress with flat shoes.

                    EMILY
          You're not that into cars, are
          you?

                    JOHN
          What do you mean?

                    EMILY
          You're leaning on it and you're
          letting me lean on it.

                    JOHN
          Yeah, so what. It's a fucking car,
          this isn't going to hurt it.

                    EMILY
          I once dated a guy in high-school
          who had a Ford Ranger, like from
          nineteen-ninety-nine. He would
          yell at me for closing the door a
          little too hard.

                    JOHN
          Yeah, you get like that whenever
          you earn something you really
          wanted. I kind of...stopped caring
          about those things...You look nice
          by the way.

                    EMILY
               (warm smile)
          Thanks, John.

Erin pulls up next to them in her Ford Escape. She's in
dress pants and a nice blouse.

                    EMILY (CONT'D)
          Are you guys completely unaware of
          how to dress for clubs or just
          that old?

John looks down at his outfit. Erin runs to hug Emily.

                    ERIN
          It makes me so happy that you came
          out here with me tonight!

                    EMILY
          I'm glad we can help!

Erin hugs John tightly but he only awkwardly pats her back.
Erin pulls away with a smile.

                    ERIN
          Wow, nice car.

                    JOHN
          Thanks. So what's the plan?

                    EMILY
          To get Erin laid! Woo-hoo!

Emily laughs. Erin puts her arms up and starts cheering
with Emily.

                    ERIN
          Yeah, woo-hoo!

They head to Club Ruby.

EXT. CLUB RUBY - NIGHT

Emily talks to Erin while John walks behind them. They wait
shortly in the line to get in.

                    EMILY
          So why do you need our help?

                    ERIN
          Well, you're gorgeous, and you're
          a guy so I figured one or both of
          you could help me somehow. Plus, I
          want us all to be friends!

Emily is warmed by the thought.

The BOUNCER looks at the three like they're an odd crowd,
he looks at Emily.

                    BOUNCER
          Can I see your I.D's?

Erin and John are flattered.

                    JOHN
          Oh my god, seriously? Thank you.

                    ERIN
               (laughing)
          Wow, thank you!

                    EMILY
          Don't worry guys, it's just me and
          a lifetime of good skin routines.

                    JOHN
               (monotone)
          Shut up. Don't ruin this for me.

Emily laughs and nudges his arm.

INT. CLUB RUBY - NIGHT

Erin goes to a high table with three chairs. They all sit
down.

                    JOHN
          I can go get drinks if you want
          while you guys talk about your
          stuff.

                    ERIN
          That's so nice, John!

                    EMILY
          Ooh! Can you just get me a vodka
          cranberry?

                    JOHN
          Sure.
               (looks to Erin)

                    ERIN
          You know what, I'll have the same.
          Thank you, John.

                    EMILY
          Thanks!

John leaves to the bar.

                    EMILY (CONT'D)
          Want me to talk to some guys for
          you?

                    ERIN
          Well, I've never had a one night
          stand before, I don't really know
          how they go...I want the
          confidence to talk to someone and
          have them instantly like me.

                    EMILY
          That's hard for anyone to do
          unless you're Emma Watson.

Erin gets a little anxious over her evening plans that may
not go as planned. Emily tries to cheer her up.

                    EMILY (CONT'D)
          We'll try to flirt some and see if
          a guy takes the bait! If not, try
          a different bait I guess.

The girls laugh.

                    ERIN
          How's my outfit? Do you think men
          will like it?

                    EMILY
          Honestly, it looks like you just
          got out of your office job and men
          probably aren't going to see you
          as a... willing target, but maybe
          if we talk to them.
               (eyes sprout open from
                an idea)
          We can make John flirt with you
          while another man is talking to
          you!

                    ERIN
          That's not a bad idea!

Erin tries to make more cleavage happen with her blouse.

John comes back with drinks.

                    EMILY
          Wow, that was fast.

Emily sips her drink while Erin adjusts her shirt.

                    JOHN
          I know the bartender and owner
          well. I did a marketing campaign
          for this place when it first
          opened.

                    EMILY
          Oh, so you get free drinks?

                    JOHN
          No, but I actually get served in a
          decent amount of time.

Emily looks at Erin and finally gets another idea.

                    EMILY
          Let's go switch outfits in the
          bathroom.

                    ERIN
          What? I can't fit in that?

                    EMILY
          Yes you can!

                    ERIN
          I'm a good twenty pounds on you.

                    EMILY
          It matters what you wear, not how
          you look in it. A guy sees a
          short, red dress and he gets to
          tell his friends he banged a girl
          in a short, red dress.

Even though John isn't a part of their conversation, he
listens and partially nods along like Emily has a point.

                    EMILY (CONT'D)
          C'mon. Let's go!

Emily takes Erin by the arm.

                    ERIN
          You don't mind?

                    EMILY
          I said I wanted to do something
          crazy, and to me this is crazy,
          let's go!

INT. CLUB RUBY BATHROOM - NIGHT

Emily undresses in the bathroom stall while Erin changes
outside of it. Emily looks down at her scars and frowns
then tosses her dress over the stall.

Erin throws her blouse over the stall. The OTHER WOMEN in
the bathroom pay no attention to them.

>   ERIN
> Have you had a one night stand
> before?

Emily touches the long scar on her rib.

>   EMILY
> No, I'm not comfortable enough for
> that kind of stuff, you know, with
> strangers seeing me all nude. I've
> always thought it would be fun to
> do though.

Emily slips the blouse on.

>   ERIN
> Awe, that's a shame, Emily. You
> should try and have one tonight
> too.

>   EMILY
>   (laughing)
> Maybe. I don't know.

Erin takes off her pants and hands them to Emily over the
stall.

INT. CLUB RUBY - NIGHT

Erin and Emily return to their table. John notices the
switch.

>   JOHN
> That outfit looks great Erin, you
> have nothing to worry about.

Erin blushes and wipes her hands down the side of her
dress.

>   ERIN
> Thanks. I'm not used to anything
> this tight or short but I like the
> change.

Emily's new blouse and pants fit a little loose.

>   EMILY
> Did you want to try and dance?

>   ERIN
> I'm trying to draw men near me,
> not away.

                    EMILY
          Okay, well, we should go up to
          some people then. Join their
          tables.

                    ERIN
          Seriously?

                    EMILY
          I don't know, I'm learning as I go
          too. Are you okay with sitting
          here, John?

                    JOHN
          Yeah. I can hold down the fort.
          Let me know if you need me for
          anything. I'll be here.

Emily starts to walk away but Erin leans over to John and
whispers something in his ear.

                    ERIN
          If tonight doesn't work out, did
          you want to be my back up?

John chokes on his whiskey and coke from the random
question.

                    JOHN
          I...uh. I don't know if I would
          count since I'm not a stranger.

John sees the desperation in her eyes.

                    JOHN (CONT'D)
          But we'll see how the night plays
          out.

                    ERIN
               (excited)
          You're a good friend, John!

Erin catches up to Emily.

                    ERIN (CONT'D)
          Is it weird we didn't switch
          shoes?

                    EMILY
          No, your heels go better anyway.

INT. CLUB RUBY - NIGHT

Emily walks towards three men, ZACH, AARON, and GABE (all
25, average build) Zach and Aaron are the normal ones while
Gabe just has the look of crazy in his eyes. The men are in
a booth with a pitcher of beer.

Emily talks louder and is more excited about everything to
seem drunker. She tussles her hair a little.

                    EMILY
          Hey, do you mind if we join? This
          place is super crowded.

                    ZACH
          Hell yeah, take a seat!

Emily motions Erin into the booth first. Emily pushes Erin
into the booth more and more so she's closer to Gabe.

                    EMILY
          So hey, how's it going? I'm Emily.
          This is my friend, Erin.

                    AARON
          My name is Aaron too!

                    ZACH
          I'm Zach.

                    GABE
          I'm Gabe, how's it going?

Gabe reaches out to shake the girls' hands.

                    ZACH
          Gabe, don't be weird man, why you
          gotta shake hands?

                    AARON
          Yeah, this isn't a job interview,
          what the fuck?

Zach and Aaron laugh.

                    ZACH
          Would you gals like anything to
          drink?

                    EMILY
          Oh my gosh, that's so nice of you!

Zach waves his hands for the waitress, TAYLOR (25). Taylor
is tall and slim with thick, blonde hair. She's in a black,
skimpy dress.

                    AARON
          What brings you ladies out here?

                    EMILY
          I'm just taking her out for her
          birthday.

                    GABE
          How old did you turn?

Erin chokes up a little.

                    EMILY
          Thirty-five.

                    AARON
          What? That's crazy! You don't look
          that old.

                    ERIN
          Probably just my dress.
               (awkward laughing)

                    AARON
          You look great. Happy birthday!

                    ERIN
               (flattered)
          Thank you.

Taylor walks over with a tray and a shot of whiskey already
on it.

                    ZACH
               (to Taylor)
          Can we get another pitcher with
          two more glasses?

                    TAYLOR
          Of course, honey.

Emily watches Taylor walk over to John who touches his
shoulder and sets down the whiskey shot from her tray.

John and Taylor smile at each other and start having a
conversation. Emily has never seen him smile that much when
he talked to anybody. Emily turns her attention back to her
new friends.

                    EMILY
          So what brings you guys here
          tonight?

                    ZACH
          Break up. So just celebrating a
          night out finally.

Everyone laughs.

                    EMILY
          I think I see an old friend up at
          the bar, I'll be right back!

Emily leaves Erin with the men and walks swiftly past John
at the table. He swallows the whiskey shot given to him by
Taylor. Emily motions at him.

                    EMILY (CONT'D)
          Hurry up and meet me at the bar!

John looks at all the drinks on the table.

                    EMILY (CONT'D)
          Forget about our drinks just come
          up here!

INT. CLUB RUBY TABLE - NIGHT

Erin is alone with the boys. She sees her friend DEMI (40,
slightly overweight and who likes to pretend she still has
her youth). Demi and Erin greet each other with hugs.

                    ERIN
          Demi! Crazy seeing you here
          tonight! I'm taking a few new
          members out, they're helping me
          with my list!

                    DEMI
          Hey, sweetie! That's awesome! I
          didn't know we had new members
          yet?

                    ERIN
          No, not yet, they still might not
          want the help, but I really hope
          they do. They are both still
          getting used to meetings and their
          list. They both seem so nice!

                    DEMI
          I can't wait to meet them at the
          church, I'll leave you alone for
          your list though, have fun, love
          you!

Demi and Erin hug. Demi waves at the three boys and walks the other way. Erin sits back down.

INT. CLUB RUBY BAR - NIGHT

Emily waits at the bar for John to come up behind her.

Taylor puts clean glasses away from behind the bar.

                    EMILY
          Okay, look. I'm going to take our
          cocktails and say they're from
          you. Just try to periodically
          flirt on Erin throughout the
          night. Send drinks maybe, because
          these guys are boring and aren't
          going to take any hints. Okay? And
          then just wave or wink so they can
          see you too.

                    JOHN
          Copy that.

Taylor interjects their conversation.

                    TAYLOR
          John, back up here already?

                    JOHN
          No, I'm just meeting up with a
          friend. I'll take another round
          whenever you get the chance
          though.

                    TAYLOR
          Anything for you Johnny!
               (winks)

Emily turns away from the bar and rolls her eyes at Taylor.
She grabs the two cranberry vodkas from her old table.

INT. CLUB RUBY - NIGHT

Emily sets the drinks down and the three boys are confused.

                    EMILY
          Oh my gosh, Erin, this really nice
          guy up at the bar got us drinks.

                    ERIN
          Really? Who?

                              EMILY
                    He said his name was John.

Emily points at John so all the men and Erin stare. John
does finger guns at Erin which makes Emily bring her face
to her hands for how embarrassing John is at flirting.

                              AARON
                    Well, here's some beer, feel free
                    to drink with us too whenever we
                    get more glasses.

                              ERIN
                    Thanks, guys. Of course, you're
                    fun! I like you guys!

Zach pours more beer in his glass.

                              ZACH
                    Got anything you want to cheers
                    to?

                              ERIN
                    Youth, I guess.
                         (laughing)

Taylor drops off a long island iced tea.

                              TAYLOR
                    This one is for you, from John,
                    he's over there.

Taylor leaves and everyone looks over at John again. John
waves fast then holds up a "call me" sign and smiles.

                              AARON
                    Sheesh, what a creeper. He just
                    bought you guys three drinks in
                    the last minute.

                              ZACH
                    Right, like buy one drink and
                    they'll let you know if they're
                    interested.

                              GABE
                    That guy just looks like a tool.

                              AARON
                    If he bothers you ladies just let
                    us know.

Emily reaches across the table to touch Aaron's arm.

                    EMILY
          Awe, you guys are so sweet, thank
          you.

                    ERIN
          You guys want this?

                    AARON
          No. But drink it, it's free!
          Consider it a birthday gift.

                    GABE
          Any plans of birthday sex?

Emily and Erin look at each other. Emily takes Erin by the
arm and drags her out of the booth.

                    EMILY
          It was nice talking to you guys
          but I think we're gonna go dance
          now.

Erin follows Emily.

                    ERIN
          Why are we leaving?

                    EMILY
          We're just getting away from the
          weird one. If Zach or Aaron wants
          you, they'll come up to you.

                    ERIN
          Oh. Okay!

INT. CLUB RUBY TABLE - NIGHT

Emily and Erin sit at their original table with John.

                    JOHN
          So how'd it go? Did I help?

                    EMILY
          I told you to wave not do finger
          guns!

                    JOHN
          Hey, I waved too. You said wave or
          wink and I'm not a winker.

                    ERIN
          Yeah, but then you waved like you
          were swatting mosquitoes at a
          cookout with Freddie Mercury!

                    JOHN
                 (laughing)
          I was just trying to make sure
          they saw me.

                    EMILY
          I think someone's a little tipsy.

                    JOHN
          Perhaps...

John slides his whiskey and coke past three other empty
glasses to Emily. Aaron comes up to their table.

                    AARON
          Hey, sorry to interrupt but I'm
          actually about to take off now
          without them. If you guys need a
          nearly sober driver, I can take
          you home.

Erin and Emily share a happy glare.

                    ERIN
          Yeah! I would like to leave too.

                    AARON
          Really? Okay!

Emily brings Erin closer to her.

                    EMILY
          Just don't chicken out! Call me if
          things get weird. And don't worry
          about getting the dress dirty, I
          borrowed it from a friend a long
          time ago! Just have fun.

                    ERIN
          You got it.
                 (to Aaron)
          She's going to stay behind, is
          that okay?

                    AARON
          Yeah. Sure.

Erin and Aaron leave with smiles.

                    EMILY
          Wow. That went faster than I
          thought it would.

                    JOHN
          I'm not surprised.

                    EMILY
          Well, our little girl is all grown
          up. Want to stay or leave?

                    JOHN
          Let me sober up first.

                    EMILY
          Well if we wait for that I can
          just drive!

                    JOHN
          I don't want to sound like that
          guy who cares too much about his
          car but that was still forty
          thousand I dropped down on it.

                    EMILY
          Awe, please! I'll be super
          careful.

                    JOHN
          It's a stick, you realize that
          right? Do you know how to drive a
          manual?

                    EMILY
          I'm a fast learner!

EXT. EMPTY PARKING LOT - NIGHT

Emily messes with the radio while John drives his Audi into
a parking lot. Emily is scared at first.

                    EMILY
          Why are we here right now?

                    JOHN
          What do you mean? This is where
          you're getting murdered.

                    EMILY
          What?

                    JOHN
          You want to learn stick or not?

                    EMILY
          Seriously? Yes!

Emily takes her seat belt off and rushes out her door. She
jumps over and slides over the hood.

                    JOHN
          Hey! Chill, woman!
               (to himself)
          Shit, maybe I do care about this
          car.

Emily opens up the driver door.

                    EMILY
          Get out already!

                    JOHN
          I'm coming.

John puts the car in neutral and pulls the emergency break
up. He gets out of the car and walks behind to the
passenger side.

                    EMILY
          How do you move the seat up?

                    JOHN
          Side. Now push the clutch down and
          release the emergency brake. Then
          move it into first and do the
          gradual catch-release everyone
          talks about.

Emily thinks about it and starts her attempt. The car jumps
and shuts off.

                    EMILY
          What happened?!

                    JOHN
          You stalled it.

                    EMILY
          Now what.

                    JOHN
          Usually, you get honked at, people
          laugh at you.

                    EMILY
          Why'd it stall?

                    JOHN
          You weren't giving it enough gas.
          Now to start it, push the clutch
          while you turn the key.

                    EMILY
          Do I have to put it in neutral
          because I think it's in first?

                    JOHN
          No, when you push the clutch in
          that makes the transmission go
          into neutral...Just don't be
          afraid to give it more gas.

Emily does as he says but pushes hard on the gas and floors
the Audi. The car goes.

                    JOHN (CONT'D)
          Too much gas! It's gradual!

John's hands cling to the handle and seat. Emily screams
and laughs. The car stalls again because she doesn't give
it more gas.

                    EMILY
          Why'd it stop again?

                    JOHN
          You have to keep giving it gas. If
          you don't, push in the clutch so
          it doesn't stall.

                    EMILY
          This is making my head hurt.

                    JOHN
          Just stay there, I'm coming
          around.

John makes his way around the car and opens the driver side
door.

                    JOHN (CONT'D)
          You want to sit on my lap or just
          watch my feet?

                    EMILY
          You are really determined to help
          me, aren't you?

                    JOHN
          It's on my Marigold list now.

The two laugh and Emily gets out.

John moves his seat back.

Emily plants herself on his lap.

                    EMILY
          Seat-belts!

Emily starts to buckle the two of them into one seat but
John takes it from her.

                    JOHN
          Yeah, let's not do that.

John grabs her hips to move her over slightly.

                    JOHN (CONT'D)
          Sorry, I actually need to see, I'm
          not going to let myself hit the
          one fucking pole in the parking
          lot. Now just rest your feet on
          top of mine.

John puts his hand on the shifter and Emily puts her hand
on top of his.

                    JOHN (CONT'D)
          Now try to pay attention to what I
          do while also not letting us hit
          anything.

John and Emily have a great time of just going up and down
gears one and two. She starts to get the hang of it but
it's funny whenever she doesn't.

                    EMILY
          Can you do a donut?!

                    JOHN
          We can try, this has traction
          control though, no promises.

John tries to pull off a donut that isn't half bad but
Emily still has fun with it.

John stops the car but their laughs continue. They smile
wide, Emily looks back to John and they have intense eye
contact.

EXT. EMILY'S APARTMENT BUILDING PARKING LOT - NIGHT

John parks his car.

                    EMILY
          I hope Erin's doing okay.

                    JOHN
          I'm sure she is.

                    EMILY
          Tonight was so much fun. I really
          don't want it to end. I can't
          remember the last time I've been
          so spontaneous and carefree.

                    JOHN
          Yeah, me too. But it doesn't have
          to end just because we're home.

                    EMILY
          Yeah? What would you want to do?

                    JOHN
          I have alcohol. I have a TV. I'm
          sure a lot of the same things your
          apartment does.

                    EMILY
               (smiling, laughing)
          Let's go check it out then.

INT. JOHN'S APARTMENT - NIGHT

John unlocks his door and lets Emily walk through first.

                    EMILY
          Wow, it's nice here.

                    JOHN
          Yeah. Just a bunch of stuff that I
          was allowed to keep. Want me to
          make you something or you want a
          beer?

Emily takes a deep breath and quickly turns around. She
steps into John and simply kisses his lips. He immediately
kisses back. Their lips stay locked together as he moves
her to his bedroom.

INT. JOHN'S BEDROOM - NIGHT

John takes off his unbuttoned shirt and his white T-shirt
is left on. He tries to take off Emily's blouse but she
pulls it back down.

                    JOHN
          What's wrong? Are you okay with
          this?

                    EMILY
          I just...I haven't done this in a
          while...

                    JOHN
              (confused at what she
              means)
          Do you want to go slower then?

Emily hesitates.

                    JOHN (CONT'D)
              (joking)
          I'm a stranger, this should be
          easy!

He grabs around her waist and pulls her closer. Her hands
go on top of his.

                    EMILY
              (blunt, disappointed)
          I just have scars. They're
          embarrassing.

                    JOHN
          So. That's not weird. It happens.
          If it makes you feel better I'm
          not going to be looking at them.

Emily laughs and he takes her shirt off the rest of the
way. John cups her breast with one hand then kisses it. She
has long vertical scars on her side that he doesn't pay
attention to.

He brings his head back up but his eyes stare at her
breasts in the black bra.

                    JOHN (CONT'D)
          Yeah, I don't know what you're
          talking about.

Emily laughs and they fall on the bed together.

INT. JOHN'S BEDROOM - NIGHT

John and Emily sleep in his bed with only sheets on them.
Emily sleeps away from John. Her phone on the nightstand
wakes her up. It's a text from Erin:

"Last night was perfect!! I'm sneaking out of his house
now!! Sorry if I wake you, see you Tuesday!"

A smile grows on Emily's face and she laughs. She puts her
phone down and cuddles up to John and falls back asleep.

INT. EMILY'S APARTMENT LIVING ROOM - DAY

Emily sits on her couch in pajamas with Paul. She crosses
off "Do something crazy" on her list. She starts fiddling
with her phone. She looks at John's contact. A text comes
up from Claire:

"Haven't heard from you in forevs, Myah and I are getting
coffee in a few if you want to join."

Emily ignores the text. She puts her phone down. Her phone
starts to ring and she rolls her eyes at the thought of it
being Claire but perks up when she sees it's from John.

She lets it ring a few times and doesn't let any of the
excitement escape when she answers it.

                    EMILY
          Hello?

INTERCUT:

JOHN'S APARTMENT BATHROOM - SAME

John has a damp towel around his waist from the shower.

                    JOHN
          You should get yourself checked.

                    EMILY
          What!?

                    JOHN
          I'm just fucking with you. What's
          up?

                    EMILY
               (rolling her eyes)
          You are not funny. How do I know
          you're kidding?

                    JOHN
          Emily, I have nice enough health
          insurance that if I had concerns I
          wouldn't be afraid to go.

                    EMILY
          That's actually very convincing.
          So what's up with you?

                    JOHN
          I was just wondering if you'd like
          to go on a date sometime?

                    EMILY
          I would love to!

                    JOHN
          Great. I'll think of a place. Want
          to go next week?

                    EMILY
          Like Saturday night?

                    JOHN
          Sure.

                    EMILY
          Totally! I'll see you before then
          right, at Marigold?

                    JOHN
          Yeah, I guess.

                    EMILY
               (grinning)
          Cool, see ya then.

                    JOHN
          Yeah, see you later.

Emily hangs up and smiles. She pulls out her list and
stares at it. She crosses out "Fall in love" then cuddles
up with Paul.

EXT. SUNFLOWER/FLOWER FIELD - DAY

Abe and Emily are in the middle of a giant sunflower field,
ready to pick the best flowers. There is a mix of many
colorful flowers like marigolds, tulips, and sunflowers.
Abe has a sun hat and garden gloves on. He holds a basket
and garden scissors.

                    EMILY
          I let my old friends go like you
          mentioned and it actually feels
          kind of good.

                    ABE
          I could tell they weren't good
          friends for you just by how you
          carried yourself. You look more
          radiant every time I see you.

Emily smiles and blushes.

                    ABE (CONT'D)
          So, Erin was telling me about your
          night out at our Monday meeting.

                    EMILY
          Oh my gosh, that was like the best
          night ever!

                    ABE
          Yeah, she asked me to pick her up
          at four in the morning then said
          she wanted to wait until next
          meeting to tell us all about it.
          What did you do while she was at
          that man's house?

                    EMILY
          Oh, that's kind of funny. Since
          John went with us, I ended up
          hanging out with him.

                    ABE
          Yeah? How'd that go? I get a good
          vibe from John.

                    EMILY
          Really! Oh, that's great to hear
          from you! I was going to ask you
          what you thought of him.

Abe snips a sunflower stem and places it in his basket.

                    ABE
          We've only known each other for a
          short while, but I only want the
          best for you, Emily.
               (he looks at the small
                flowers)
          Do you think Whitney would like
          the tiger lily or tulips more?

                    EMILY
          Why don't you pick her some
          marigolds? You know, to remind her
          of the help group.

                    ABE
               (he thinks about it)
          I like that idea.

He snips two red marigold flowers.

Emily tries to say something but stops herself to think
more about it.

                    EMILY
              (beat)
          Can I show you something?

                    ABE
          Of course, anything.

                    EMILY
          Can I show you my scars? I'm
          really insecure about them and I
          just wish I wasn't holding onto
          them anymore.

                    ABE
          That's real brave of you. You
          can't get rid of your scars, so
          you have to carry them with you,
          it's best to make peace with them.

Emily smiles. She looks around for people but the tall
sunflowers hide her from anyone that would be around. Emily
lifts one side of her shirt up.

Abe bends over to look at them. He pushes her shirt up more
with his hand to look at them more closely.

                    ABE (CONT'D)
          Amazing. You can tell which ones
          are from kitchen knives, pocket
          knives, and razors.

                    EMILY
          Yeah, they've kept me from having
          many boyfriends and going to the
          beach and stuff.

                    ABE
          Thank you for being comfortable
          enough to show me.

Emily is hesitant to say what's on her mind again but says
it anyway.

                    EMILY
          So, if I'm still unhappy by the
          date on my Marigold list, then
          what?

                    ABE
          I really don't want you to take
          your life without trying to do
          what you've always wanted to do.
              (MORE)

                    ABE (CONT'D)
          By the end of October, if you
          think killing yourself is the only
          thing that can make you happy, I
          say go for it.

Emily is surprised by the crazy advice.

                    EMILY
          Seriously?

Emily starts to like the unconventional idea just because
it's Abe's.

                    ABE
          Yes. You have a couple months to
          do everything selfishly to make
          yourself happy. Similar to living
          like you were dying. We can always
          extend the date but it's just a
          guilt-free way of killing
          yourself, because face it, you've
          tried everything else. I believe
          you should do whatever it takes to
          make yourself happy. You know
          what's best for yourself.
          Sometimes you have to be selfish.

Emily nods as she adapts to the idea.

                    EMILY
          Yeah, you're right.

                    ABE
          I've seen too many of my bunkmates
          suffer in pain. They stayed alive
          just because they were begged to.

Abe snips a sunflower and a tiger lily.

INT. FLOWER SHOP - DAY

Abe puts his basket of flowers on the cashier's counter.

The CASHIER takes the flowers out and wraps them in a
bouquet.

                    ABE
          Thanks for coming and helping me
          today. I think Whitney is going to
          love these for our anniversary.

                EMILY
It was no problem at all! Thanks
for inviting me.

                ABE
Is there anything else you want to
talk about?

Emily thinks about something to see if she wants to bring
it up.

                EMILY
Well, this doesn't have anything
to do negatively with my condition
so I'm sorry if I shouldn't
mention it to you, it was more of
a conflict that I don't know how
to solve.

                ABE
Go right ahead. I'm all ears.

                EMILY
Well, after watching all of you
guys, I see how you don't really
let people walk all over you. But
my boss is doing just that. He
said he was going to split up new
work for everyone, but it turns
out it's just me doing two jobs;
not that I don't mind doing it, I
just want a raise that he refuses
to give me...So what should I do?

                ABE
Hmmm. Interesting. Would it be
okay if I mention your name and
ask what others think on this
issue so it's not just what I
think?

                EMILY
Yeah, totally!

                ABE
Where do you work? I'll talk to
him.

                EMILY
Oh that's crazy. He's a mean guy.

                ABE
I'm sure, but I would love to help
so it would be my pleasure.

The cashier hands him the bouquet and he hands her a fifty
dollar bill.

She starts to get his change. Abe picks out one of the two
red marigolds out of the bouquet.

                    ABE (CONT'D)
          Here.

He hands the flower to Emily and she gets a big smile. She
feels loved just from the small gesture.

                    ABE (CONT'D)
          I picked an extra marigold just
          for you!

                    EMILY
          Oh! Abe!

Emily holds the flower close to her heart.

INT. MARIGOLD CHURCH - NIGHT

Emily leans against the coffee table with John and Whitney.
Abe walks up to them.

                    ABE
          So Emily, before I talk to your
          boss, I'd just like to have your
          word that you want to commit to
          here as your help group. You know,
          be a real member.

                    EMILY
          Yeah, this place is really great!

                    ABE
          That's awesome to hear. What about
          you, John? Have you figured out if
          this is a good practice for you
          yet?

                    JOHN
          Yeah, it's been helping so far.

                    ABE
          I like to hear that. But are you
          going to commit? Just like
          medicine, you can't just take it
          when you want! So I'll give you
          till next class, just let me know
          if you'd like to stay here.

                    JOHN
          Okay, will do.

EXT. MARIGOLD CHURCH - NIGHT

John stands by his other car, a Chevy Impala, and Emily is
next to her less impressive car, an older Honda Civic.

                    EMILY
          So, do you really not know if
          you're going to keep coming here
          or not?

                    JOHN
          Yeah, it's just not my cup of tea.

                    EMILY
          Why not though? Everyone is so
          nice and helpful.

                    JOHN
          Yeah. It's just not my thing is
          all. I just did this for someone
          else and now I can say I tried it.

                    EMILY
          Well, we never even had the chance
          to ride together!

                    JOHN
          I guess we will just have to go
          somewhere else together.

                    EMILY
          Like on Saturday.

                    JOHN
          Exactly.

                    EMILY
          Did you decide where yet?

                    JOHN
          What kind of date did you want?

                    EMILY
          I want to try something new. I've
          never been on a real date, so that
          shouldn't be hard. But you asked
          me out, so you have to figure
          something out for us.

                    JOHN
          Oh, is that the rule now?

               EMILY
That's always been the rule!

               JOHN
Do you have a nice dress? Not like
a club dress.

               EMILY
Yeah, I have other dresses, John.

Emily kisses John on the cheek and he gets in his car.

               EMILY (CONT'D)
I'm staying here for a little.
I'll see you later.

               JOHN
            (smiling)
Oh, okay. See ya.

INT. WILLIAM & SON CAR INSURANCE - DAY

Emily walks into her cubicle and Rebecca peeks around the
corner and just stares at her.

               EMILY
Morning Rebecca...Can I help you?

               REBECCA
The envelope on your desk...it's a
check.

               EMILY
Rebecca! You can't go through my
stuff! I told you three times
already and now I'm going to David
about this.

Rebecca stays in her seat.

               REBECCA
Good luck with that.

Emily walks briskly to David's office with the envelope in
her hand.

INT. DAVID'S OFFICE - DAY

The woman that sits in David's chair is JESSICA (29).
Jessica just looks like a bitch, fried blonde hair and a
lot of makeup.

                        EMILY
          Oh. Who are you?

                        JESSICA
          Jessica, I'm covering the office
          for David today. He's in the
          hospital.

                        EMILY
          Oh my god, what happened?

                        JESSICA
          He was mugged last night.

                        EMILY
          That's terrible!

EXT. GROCERY STORE - DAY

A flashback to yesterday. It's a clear, sunny day and a few
pedestrians enter and exit the store.

David makes his way to his car in his tight suit, he has a
few groceries. When he's to his car he gets pistol-whipped
by a .40 silver S&W revolver.

EXT. GROCERY STORE ALLEY - DAY

Abe drags David behind the store while David tries to kick
away from him. His groceries stay behind.

                        DAVID
          I don't have any money!

                        ABE
          Shut the fuck up and listen.
          You're either giving Emily a raise
          for the job she does or you're
          firing her and giving her two
          months pay.

                        DAVID
          What?

                        ABE
          You know exactly who I'm talking
          about, don't play dumb!

Abe whacks the pistol across David's face again then kicks
him in the stomach.

                    DAVID
          Okay! Yes! I'll give her the
          money!

                    ABE
          No! You're giving her what she
          deserves.

A male PEDESTRIAN (50, and looks good for his age) runs to
the commotion.

                    PEDESTRIAN
          Hey! What's going on!

The pedestrian makes a happy face at Abe.

                    PEDESTRIAN (CONT'D)
          Abe?

                    ABE
          Terry!

Terry, the pedestrian, walks over to hug Abe. David is in a
fetal position with his hands over his head and breathes
heavy. David's face bleeds.

                    TERRY
          I'd recognize those Hawaiian
          shirts from anywhere! What are you
          doing?

                    ABE
          I'm helping a new member.

Terry points down at David with confusion.

                    ABE (CONT'D)
          No, this isn't the new member.

                    TERRY
          That's fantastic. Actually, I've
          always wanted to assault someone.
          Can I actually like, help you or
          something?

Abe pats Terry's back and puts his revolver away in his
pants.

                    ABE
          Of course. Go ahead and give him a
          kick! He's apparently been a real
          dick.

Terry stomps on David and he screams. He punches him over
and over again. It's sloppy because Terry's never been in a
fight before. Abe laughs along.

                    ABE (CONT'D)
          Good!

Terry backs away and laughs

                    TERRY
          Thanks, Abe.

                    ABE
          I'll see you Sunday right?

                    TERRY
          Yeah! I'll be there for the
          fundraiser next month too.

Terry leaves and FEMALE PEDESTRIAN (30) pokes her head to
see the commotion.

                    DAVID
          Someone help me!

                    TERRY
               (to Female Pedestrian)
          Don't worry about it, he deserves
          it.

Female Pedestrian walks with concern and their head down.

INT. WILLIAM & SON CAR INSURANCE - DAY

Emily stands in the doorway of David's office while Jessica
still sits at the desk.

                    EMILY
          Wow, I hope he's okay. Did they
          take much money?

                    JESSICA
          No, I guess he didn't have any on
          him, but that's just what he told
          me.

Jessica notices the envelope Emily is holding.

                    JESSICA (CONT'D)
          Oh are you Emily?

                    EMILY
          Yes.

                    JESSICA
          Great. I'm supposed to tell you
          that you're fired.

                    EMILY
          What?

                    JESSICA
          Look, that's why you have the
          envelope. I wasn't told anything
          else but to give you that and fire
          you. And take calls.

Emily stands there in shock.

                    EMILY
          Can I ask why?

The phone starts to ring and Jessica reaches for it.

                    JESSICA
          You can. But I don't know. Bye
          now.

Emily rolls her eyes and turns around.

INT. WILLIAM & SON'S CAR INSURANCE, EMILY'S CUBICLE - DAY

Emily gets her belongings at her cubicle.

                    REBECCA
          I told you good luck because
          Dave's not here. He was murdered!

                    EMILY
          He was mugged, Rebecca. Calm down.

                    REBECCA
          Okay, so you heard.

Emily starts to leave the office.

                    REBECCA (CONT'D)
               (mocking, aware that
               she's fired)
          Hey, where are you going?

Emily doesn't respond to her coworker.

EXT. WILLIAM & SON PARKING LOT - DAY

Emily takes out the papers in her open envelope. It's a
check for five-thousand dollars. There is a faint smudge of
blood on the check.

Emily holds it closer to her face but turns her attention
to the note inside. The note inside says:

"Two months in advance for the inconvenience. Please don't
show up here again. Sorry."

Emily is mad but likes having the five-thousand-dollar
severance pay.

INT. BISOU RESTAURANTE - NIGHT

John wears a nice suit and Emily is in a black dress that
only reveals her back and arms. Her hair is half up and
curled. The WAITER pours them wine.

                    WAITER
          Your entrees are almost ready.

                    JOHN
          Thanks.

The waiter leaves. Emily leans into John.

                    EMILY
          I still feel a little underdressed
          for this place.

                    JOHN
          No, not at all. You look great. I
          promise.

John takes a drink from his wine glass. Emily takes a drink
from her wine and cringes.

                    JOHN (CONT'D)
               (laughing)
          Do you not like the wine? You
          picked it.

                    EMILY
          Honestly, I just picked the
          cheapest one. Eighty dollars for a
          bottle of wine!

                    JOHN
          That's not bad for here.

                    EMILY
          Exactly! That's why this is
          ridiculous.

                    JOHN
          Emily. You're not even paying, I
          am. Would you just get whatever
          you want and not worry about it?

John starts eating the fancy bread on the table.

                    EMILY
          God, I feel terrible. Can I at
          least pay for half?

                    JOHN
               (eating bread)
          No. Fuck off.

Emily laughs.

                    JOHN (CONT'D)
          Didn't you just get fired? Save
          your money.

                    EMILY
          I'm just going back to bar-tending
          again until I find something.

                    JOHN
          Want to get a different bottle or
          a cocktail?

                    EMILY
          No, it's fine. After the first
          glass of wine, I stop tasting it.

                    JOHN
          Not a bad thing. Are you happy
          with your entree? Or did you try
          to order cheap on that too?

                    EMILY
          No, I like it, thanks.

Emily plays with her wine glass to avoid the awkward,
burning question she has.

                    EMILY (CONT'D)
          So can I ask about your ex-wife?

                    JOHN
          It wouldn't be a great date unless
          we did, right?

Emily laughs hard and reaches across the table to touch his arm.

>   EMILY
>   You crack me up, I love it. But is
>   it okay? I'm just curious, I'd
>   like to know you more...Just to
>   help with your list!

>   JOHN
>   (joking, flirting)
>   Ah. You need to know even though
>   I'm not going anymore?

>   EMILY
>   You're not going to Marigold
>   anymore?

Emily starts to eat the bread too.

John shakes his head "no".

>   JOHN
>   But, ask away. Go ahead.

>   EMILY
>   Why'd you guys split?

>   JOHN
>   She was crazy.

>   EMILY
>   Ah, that's what all exes say. What
>   really happened?

>   JOHN
>   She was a one night stand who I
>   accidentally knocked up. Then made
>   us get married so she could have
>   my money.

>   EMILY
>   You have a kid?

>   JOHN
>   Yeah, I have a four-year-old girl
>   that I was never given any custody
>   to.

>   EMILY
>   That's terrible, I'm so sorry. But
>   how'd she make you get married?

                    JOHN
She actually threatened me. She
said she'd take me to court for
raping her if I didn't marry her.

                    EMILY
Did you really take advantage of
her?

                    JOHN
No. We both had a few drinks that
night. Even though neither of us
were drunk, my lawyer said it
wouldn't hold up in court since
you can't consent under the
influence.

                    EMILY
But you were drunk too? You know
if you were pushing her for
anything at all that's not right
to do...

                    JOHN
No, she was pushing me for it,
which I was okay with. We still
messed around after that one night
anyway, but she still brought that
night up for court purposes. I
knew her from college a few years
back. I found out she set me up
for everything which is why she's
crazy.

                    EMILY
How so?

                    JOHN
She said that we had to get
married since she's pregnant and
if we didn't get married she would
take me to court for rape. I
thought she was just panicking
because she was pregnant and I
always wanted a family anyway so I
said sure.

                    EMILY
Wow...that's absolutely insane.
What was the point of doing that?

                    JOHN
So she could divorce me for
alimony.

                    EMILY
          How much does she get?

                    JOHN
          About four thousand a month.

Emily chokes a little.

                    EMILY
          Wow. That's more than I make in a
          month! Well, did.

                    JOHN
          Yeah, she purposely stayed with me
          for a couple of years so she could
          get more and then you add child
          support. But, she lets me see
          Paige once a month which is nice.
          I just hope that's where all the
          money's going.

                    EMILY
          I'm speechless. I can't believe
          someone would go to that extent.
          Like, just get a real job?

                    JOHN
          I told you, people are fucking
          crazy.

                    EMILY
          Are you and your daughter close?

                    JOHN
          She barely knows who I am. I
          raised her for three years but
          she's still young...She calls me
          dad. But, she also calls Stacey's
          boyfriend that.

                    EMILY
          Your first mistake was getting
          with someone named Stacey.

John nods his head "yes" to agree.

                    EMILY (CONT'D)
          Do you think I could visit with
          you once?

                    JOHN
               (small laughter)
          Is it because you want to see what
          my ex looks like?

                    EMILY
          A little, but I'd also like to see
          your daughter.

                    JOHN
          Yeah, she's a cutie.
               (warm smile)
          I'm supposed to see her at the end
          of this month. Stacey cancels on
          me a lot so sorry if plans fall
          through.

                    EMILY
          So, just to be clear, she found
          you years after you graduated from
          college to use you for your money?
          How'd she know you had any money?

                    JOHN
          Right after college I did well
          because I helped my friend's
          business sprout up and that's when
          I made my agency. I found out
          Stacey was actually trying to get
          with him because he was doing well
          too but he was engaged.

                    EMILY
          What was it like being married to
          her? Like in a relationship you
          hate?

                    JOHN
          It was the dumbest thing. The
          entire time I kept trying to make
          things better not realizing she
          was just using me the entire time.
          I hate myself for being so idiotic
          but it's over. Nothing me or my
          lawyer could do. His focus was on
          saving me money, not really
          justice.

Emily touches his hand.

                    EMILY
          I'm sorry. I'm glad you told me
          though. Are you still upset about
          it?

                         JOHN
          Just at myself. Plus, I just feel
          bad for the women that have
          actually been taken advantage of
          and then you have the few people
          like Stacey. But like I said, it's
          over, there's nothing else I can
          do but to get over it.

John takes more bread and eats it.

                         EMILY
          I hope you don't think I'm using
          you.

                         JOHN
          I don't think you're dumb enough
          to use a man who only makes two
          hundred grand a year. There are
          richer men out there.

                         EMILY
          Yeah, but you're pretty young.
          It's odd that you're so open with
          how much you make.

                         JOHN
          I lose almost fifty thousand a
          year because of her. If I cared
          about money anymore I probably
          would have...

John stops himself from saying more personal things. He
shakes his head.

                      JOHN (CONT'D)
          I just stopped caring about money
          and I just like what I do now. For
          the most part. I mean, I haven't
          spent money on anything except
          bills. This is actually the first
          time I've been out in a year so,
          it's a date for me too.

                         EMILY
          That's great, John.

Emily raises her wine glass to cheers with John.

                      EMILY (CONT'D)
          See, all thanks to Abe's help
          group, we met! And you're going to
          leave it!

The waiter drops off their entrees. John has a rare steak and Emily has chicken. John sees how Emily drools over his steak.

>   JOHN
>   Did you want to switch?

>   EMILY
>   What?

>   JOHN
>   You can have my steak if you want
>   it over yours, I know you tried to
>   be cheap.

>   EMILY
>   ...Okay. Yes.

John starts to slide his plate towards Emily and she smiles while handing him her chicken. Emily laughs and John smiles.

>   EMILY (CONT'D)
>   It's okay, I'll let you have a
>   bite.

INT. MARIGOLD CHURCH - NIGHT

All the seats in the church are filled except for one, where John would normally sit. Whitney hugs Abe intimately but he slightly pushes her away.

>   EMILY
>   (to Abe)
>   Hey, Abe, before we start, I was
>   just wondering. Did you talk to my
>   boss at all? Because something
>   weird happened the other day.

>   ABE
>   I did have a chat with him. Is he
>   treating you better at work?

>   EMILY
>   No, I was fired, but I was given
>   money for it. Did you know he got
>   mugged?

>   ABE
>   I didn't know he got mugged, this
>   is a safe town! But when I
>   confronted him we talked about
>   some options.

                    EMILY
          Oh. Okay. Well even though I'm
          fired, I'm kind of glad things
          worked out the way they did.

                    ABE
          Great to hear! How are things with
          John?

                    EMILY
          Good! But he isn't coming anymore.

                    ABE
          Sad shame. Maybe try to get him to
          come one last time, just so I can
          see how he's doing.

                    EMILY
          Yeah, for sure, I'll try.

EXT. MARIGOLD CHURCH- NIGHT

Emily heads to her car when Lauren, the ex-member, stops
her.

                    LAUREN
          Hey! Wait. Before you go, I want
          you to be careful.

                    EMILY
          Hi? Who are you?

                    LAUREN
          I'm not going to tell you my name
          in case you tell Abe, but for your
          safety, you should leave before
          you realize you need to leave.

Emily shakes her head in confusion.

                    LAUREN (CONT'D)
          I try to stay out front to keep
          new people from coming in but Abe
          is looking out for me.

                    EMILY
          I've never seen you before.

                    LAUREN
          Abe's coming. I tried to warn you
          three times before this but
          couldn't, just trust me. He's
          manipulative.
                              (MORE)

                         LAUREN (CONT'D)
             He was there when Marie Campbell
             killed herself. He made her do it.

Lauren takes a step towards Emily and Emily is
uncomfortable by it. Lauren talks fast

                         LAUREN (CONT'D)
             You don't know what this is yet.
             But that's because you're not in
             it, you can still leave.

Lauren sees Abe. She backs away. VERONICA (28, tall, a
little overweight) and Erin grab either side of Lauren and
are overly friendly.

                         VERONICA
             Miss you, Lauren!

                         ERIN
             How's everything going?

Lauren pushes away from the women and gets in her car. She
drives away. Abe walks up to Emily and watches Lauren
leave.

                         ABE
             Do you know her?

                         EMILY
             No, but she said she knew you.

                         ABE
             She was a member and left
             recently. I directed her to leave
             because well, she has a very
             serious mental disorder that
             requires serious drugs.

                         EMILY
             Oh, that's terrible, what's wrong?

                         ABE
             Schizophrenia. She hallucinates a
             lot. Really sad, she doesn't
             believe in medicine though. I sent
             her to a doctor, I wouldn't worry
             about her.

Abe touches Emily's shoulder and walks away.

INT. YOGA STUDIO - DAY

Veronica, Whitney, and Emily are in the midst of a yoga
class.

                    WHITNEY
          It's a lot more challenging than
          you'd think!

                    EMILY
          Yeah, this kind of hurts. But at
          least I'm finally wearing yoga
          pants for yoga reasons.

                    WHITNEY
          You'll get the hang of it soon. I
          always like to get my yoga in
          before Abe's Sunday session. How
          do you like coming on Sunday's
          too?

                    EMILY
          It really helps. I ran out of meds
          and the extra distraction each
          week really helps get my mind away
          from the dead feeling.

                    VERONICA
          Yeah, you've been looking extra
          sad lately. Anything we can help
          with?

                    WHITNEY
          You want to have a girls night?
          Let's have one after we get done
          with the group today.

                    EMILY
          That sounds fun but, I promised
          John we would hang out.

                    VERONICA
          The guy that left the group?

                    WHITNEY
          Emily, this is for your health. If
          he cared for you, he'd understand.

                    EMILY
          Yeah, you're right. He'll
          understand, he's a great guy.

                    WHITNEY
          That's wonderful! I'm happy for
          you.

INT. MARIGOLD CHURCH - DAY

Abe talks over the group while everyone starts to leave.

>   ABE
>   And don't forget about our
>   fundraiser next week, it's finally
>   here. It will be at the mall with
>   two stands.

Emily calls John off of her phone.

>   EMILY
>   Hey, I tried texting you but you
>   didn't text back.

INTERCUT:

INT. JOHN'S APARTMENT, LIVING ROOM - DAY

John sits on his couch with a laptop that has houses for sale on it.

>   JOHN
>   Yeah, I'm really sorry, I just got
>   an offer back on the house I was
>   looking at, I might be moving out
>   soon.

>   EMILY
>   Oh, that's great! I can't wait to
>   see what it looks like!

>   JOHN
>   But what's up?

>   EMILY
>   Well, Veronica and Whitney suggest
>   they give me a mental health girls
>   night out over at Whitney's place.
>   They said I look extra down in the
>   dumps lately. I'd hate to cancel
>   on us but I feel like I should do
>   this.

>   JOHN
>   Yeah, go ahead, I understand. Have
>   fun, let me know if you want to
>   come here after.

>   EMILY
>   (flirty)
>   Oh, I'm sure I will. See ya.

                    JOHN
                  (smiling)
          I'll see you later.

INT. ABE AND WHITNEY'S HOUSE - NIGHT

It's early evening and Whitney pours Veronica and Emily
some wine. Abe scurries around the house for keys and his
phone before he leaves.

                    WHITNEY
          Abe honey, where are you going?

                    ABE
          I'm taking Rob to a baseball game.

                    WHITNEY
          Oh that's great!

                    ABE
                  (to Veronica and Emily)
          Hey, any of you two like amusement
          parks? Rob and Will are going to
          try and use his handicap to cut in
          line so if you're into that, I'd
          talk to them before they go.

Abe and Whitney kiss each other on the lips real quick and
then Abe leaves the house.

                    EMILY
          So, how long have you guys been
          together?

                    WHITNEY
          I've been with him since he
          started the help group, so around
          five years?

                    EMILY
          Wow, nice.

                    VERONICA
          How come John didn't stay with the
          group?

                    EMILY
          It just wasn't his thing, he's not
          a social butterfly nor wants to be
          one anyway.

                    VERONICA
          You should try and bring him back,
          it was nice having him.

                    WHITNEY
         Yeah, we always want to help as
         many people as we can. But it's
         always ultimately up to the
         person.

They all sip their wine.

                    EMILY
         I'll ask him to come to one, for
         my sake. I've been needing this
         extra support lately.

                    VERONICA
         Are you coming to the fundraiser?
         I know you're still new so you
         don't need to or anything.

                    EMILY
         Should I try to donate?

                    WHITNEY
         Sure! It helps run our group
         throughout the week and just
         support us and mental health.

                    VERONICA
         The fundraiser at the church is
         fun though, people from all the
         other help groups come out and
         there's food and some games. We
         start at the mall then move the
         party to the church.

                    WHITNEY
         Yeah, it's just a place for
         strangers to donate and for us to
         have a little day to ourselves.

                    EMILY
         That sounds awesome, I'll totally
         be there.

                    WHITNEY
         Ooh! That reminds me, we have to
         think of what to make!

INT. MARIGOLD CHURCH - NIGHT

Emily escorts John with her to the chairs that are in a
circle.

                    ABE
          Wow, John! It's been a while, good
          to see you again.

Abe shakes John's hand then gives him a one-armed hug to
pat him on the back.

                    ABE (CONT'D)
          What made you come back?

                    JOHN
          Emily wanted me to come here; try
          it out again.

                    ABE
          Nice! Thanks for coming and Emily,
          for you trying to help out John.

Emily is flattered.

                    EMILY
          Oh! Abe, here, I forgot to give
          you it last week, you know, for
          helping with everything and the
          fundraiser.

Emily pulls out a check from her purse for one-thousand
dollars.

John's eyes widen, Abe smiles.

                    ABE
          Thanks so much, Emily, what a
          great contribution.

He touches Emily's shoulder and she flutters. John doesn't
like it. Abe and John share glares. Abe smirks at him.

                    ABE (CONT'D)
          You're amazing. I'll see you guys
          in three minutes when we start the
          meeting.

Abe walks away and folds the check into his pocket.

                    EMILY
          Sucks it's Tuesday, usually on
          Sundays Whitney will do this
          guided meditation thing, it's so
          relaxing.

                    JOHN
              (to himself, confused)
          Sundays now?
                    (MORE)

                    JOHN (CONT'D)
               (to Emily)
          Why the hell do you guys do that
          here?

                    EMILY
          We did it in yoga and she thought
          it would be a great idea to bring
          it to the group.

                    JOHN
          Have you missed any of these
          meetings since you've joined?

                    EMILY
          Only one, but Abe doesn't
          appreciate it when that happens so
          I really try not to.

People take their seats.

                    EMILY (CONT'D)
          See John, there's Rob, Abe, and
          now Will, so you could have guy
          friends here.

Emily takes John's hand and sits him in a chair next to
her. There are eleven people in the circle and no missing
chairs. Abe watches John's judgmental eyes that scan the
room.

Abe gets up, he grabs a coffee and brings it over to John
before he starts the meeting.

                    ABE
          Here's some coffee, John. Again,
          welcome back.

Everyone mumbles among themselves. Abe sits down and
everyone gets quiet.

                    ABE (CONT'D)
          Alright everybody, so let's start
          with the partner work we did over
          the weekend.

INT. MARIGOLD CHURCH BATHROOM - NIGHT

John tosses his empty coffee cup in the bathroom trash. Abe
walks into the bathroom with a smug face. John starts to
head to the urinal but Abe pushes John's face into the
wall.

                         JOHN
           What the fuck are you doing?

John is too confused to fight back.

                         ABE
           After today don't come back here.
           Do you hear me? You can take your
           bullshit elsewhere.

                         JOHN
                (confused, freaked out)
           What are you talking about?

                         ABE
           You don't take this seriously so
           you don't get the privilege of
           being here, got it?

                         JOHN
           Okay?

Abe turns John around and twists his arm.

                         JOHN (CONT'D)
           OW!

                         ABE
           Do you understand that you're not
           welcome here or allowed to talk
           about it?

John throws a punch but Abe blocks it.

                         JOHN
           Yes, just fuck off, psycho!

                         ABE
           Good.

Abe backs off and leaves the restroom. John brushes himself
off.

                         JOHN
           What the fuck, man.

John hesitates to go to the urinal, confused still. He
unzips his pants and takes a quick look behind him before
he starts peeing.

                         JOHN (CONT'D)
                (to himself)
           Christ, you don't do that in a
           fucking bathroom.

EXT. MARIGOLD CHURCH - NIGHT

John and Emily are at their cars.

                    JOHN
          Hey, want to come back to the new
          house? I think we should talk.

                    EMILY
          Oh, John, I really wish I could
          but I already promised to hang out
          with Whitney after this and I
          don't want to do that to her.

                    JOHN
          Okay, that's fine but we should
          really talk sometime soon.

                    EMILY
          John, what's the matter?

                    JOHN
          Emily, look...I think it's pretty
          obvious this place isn't as
          healthy as you think.

                    EMILY
               (defensive)
          What the hell does that mean?

                    JOHN
          I think this place is some sort of
          cult. They're not really trying to
          help you.

                    EMILY
          How could you say that? I haven't
          had a suicidal thought or even
          harmed myself since I joined! How
          could you say that?

John steps closer and tries to touch her but she takes a
step back.

                    JOHN
          Emily, I'm just trying to look out
          for you. I talked to Abe and he
          said he didn't want me to be here
          because I don't fit in, but what
          help group kicks people away?

                         EMILY
          Well, he's only going to try and
          help if you're willing to help
          yourself first. Take the first
          step already John, I can help you
          get there.

                         JOHN
          Trust me, Abe made it pretty clear
          he didn't want me around here
          again.

Emily scolds him.

                         JOHN (CONT'D)
          Emily, listen to me. Forget them.
          I actually really care about you,
          this place is a fucking cult! You
          need to leave before you're sucked
          in and he doesn't let you leave.

Emily doesn't like him telling her what to do.

                         EMILY
          I don't want to leave! Even if it
          is a cult, I don't care! Because
          this is the best thing that's ever
          happened to me. If you loved me,
          you'd support that.

John is speechless at first. He wants to end the argument
so he lets her win.

                         JOHN
          Fine. I'll support whatever you
          do.

                         EMILY
          Thank you.

Emily stands on her tip toes to kiss him.

                         JOHN
          Let me know when you're done doing
          whatever with Whitney, you know
          where I'll be. If you call me
          tonight, call my landline, I want
          to see if it works.

                         EMILY
                    (laughs)
          Why do you have to be an old man?

John kisses her before he leaves. He pretends he's fine and
done with this conversation.

                        JOHN
              See you.

As John and Emily separate, Abe is seen lurking a bit
further back. Emily walks to Whitney.

                        WHITNEY
              Awe, you guys are such cuties. I
              wish Abe would be that
              affectionate with me.

The two laugh. Abe walks in between them and gently pushes
Emily away from Whitney. Emily walks backward.

                        EMILY
                   (laughing)
              Oh, Abe, how can I help you?

He touches Emily's shoulder and takes her hands.

                        ABE
              Emily, you've shown so much
              progress lately and I'd really
              like you to be recognized for
              that. I'd like you to help lead
              the fundraiser with me.

                        EMILY
                   (big smile, speechless)
              Oh my gosh, Abe! I would love to,
              thank you so much! I wouldn't even
              be here if it weren't for you
              guys. This is such an honor!
                   (beat)
              You saved me, Abe.

                        ABE
                   (grinning)
              I know.

Abe and Emily hug. He pulls away to speak.

                        ABE (CONT'D)
              One more thing, I don't want you
              seeing John again.

                        EMILY
              What?

                        ABE
              You need to break up with John.

                        EMILY
                   (beat, thinking)
              Oh..okay...why?

> ABE
> I'm surprised you even have to
> ask. You know I know what's best
> for you.

Abe still has her hands. Whitney puts her hand on Abe's
shoulder and then her other hand on Emily's shoulder.

> ABE (CONT'D)
> He doesn't take this seriously.
> Therefore, he doesn't take you
> seriously.

> EMILY
> Yeah, you're right, I see what you
> mean.
> (beat)
> Thank you.

Abe walks away. Emily is not phased by his demands.

> WHITNEY
> Yeah, Abe's right. I don't trust
> John, he doesn't seem as good as
> you think. Are you ready to go?

> EMILY
> Yeah.

INT. ACE MARKETING FIRM - DAY

John sits at his desk and calls Emily on his cell phone but
she never picks up so he leaves a message.

> JOHN
> Emily, what's going on? You
> haven't talked to me since
> Tuesday, just text me back at
> least so I know you're alright.

He hangs up and sighs out of frustration.

INT. DOCTOR'S EXAMINING ROOM - DAY

Emily sits alone in the examining room. She listens to
John's voicemail and deletes it right before Doctor
Burkhart enters.

> DOCTOR BURKHART
> Hey Emily, how's it going?

> EMILY
> Good, good.

Doctor Burkart sits.

                    DOCTOR BURKHART
          You try out any group therapy
          sessions?

                    EMILY
          Yeah, I go to one at Marigold
          church. It's Tuesdays, Thursdays,
          and Sundays.

                    DOCTOR BURKHART
          Is that a local one? I haven't
          heard of that one in the registry?

                    EMILY
          Yeah, it's right downtown.

                    DOCTOR BURKHART
          What do you guys do there?

                    EMILY
          We just talk. And then we try to
          help each other out with things
          we've always wanted to do. Like, I
          helped one girl get laid and a
          handicap kid steal Ray-Bans! It's
          a nice distraction.

                    DOCTOR BURKHART
          Yeah, uh huh...that group sounds a
          little different than what I
          meant. I was talking about group
          therapy but this seems to be you
          guys getting together. But, as
          long as it's working for you.

                    EMILY
          Yeah, I think it is. Whenever I'm
          feeling down they are there to
          hang out with me. Plus, they
          understand. We get each other and
          how we feel.

                    DOCTOR BURKHART
          It's important to keep your
          individuality during these times
          because it's easy to want to move
          into a group for some sense
          of belonging. That's how people
          can influence you. It's free
          right?

                    EMILY
          Yeah. They do donations and
          fundraisers.

                    DOCTOR BURKHART
          Hm, okay. Well, I've never heard
          of the group you're in. That's not
          how the other groups usually do it
          but if this one is working for you
          then good.

INT. DOCTOR'S OFFICE HALLWAY - DAY

Doctor Burkhart hands Emily her discharge papers.

                    DOCTOR BURKHART
          Like I said, if you start getting
          symptoms and don't think the group
          therapy is helping any more, just
          make a visit. We can usually do
          same day.

Doctor Burkhart shakes Emily's hand and walks away.

INT. CHURCH BASEMENT - NIGHT

The majority of the fundraiser is over. There are close to
one hundred and fifty people shoved in the church basement.

Emily stands next to Abe. New members SKYLAR (15, female),
ANDREW (35, male), and ADRIANNE (53, female) stand with
Emily and Abe with big smiles.

                    ABE
          We had a great fundraiser, we got
          over ten thousand dollars, you
          guys are amazing! We couldn't have
          done it without our new members
          who I'd like to introduce. I know
          we're all here at different days
          and times but we are one big
          family so we should know each
          other as one.

Emily, Skylar, Andrew, and Adrianne stand in a line next to
each other.

                    ABE (CONT'D)
        So much progress in these last
        three months, four months for one
        of you, and I would like to
        finally welcome you all in as
        members of the Marigold group.
        You've earned it by helping
        someone else's life which makes
        yours worth living.

Abe shows off the new members.

                    ABE (CONT'D)
        Here is Adrianne, Andrew, Skylar,
        and Emily!

The crowd starts to clap. All the new members have happy
tears in their eyes. Skylar waves at everyone. Emily has
the widest smile.

EXT. JOHN'S NEW HOUSE - NIGHT

John's house is big with a nice driveway and path to the
front door.

Emily knocks on John's door. He opens the door. He's
excited to see her but is still upset with her.

                    JOHN
        Emily? You're here?

                    EMILY
        I know. I'm sorry. I just want to
        talk.

                    JOHN
        Oh. Okay, well, come on in.

Emily stands on her tip toes to kiss John and then hugs
him. He hugs back and picks her body up to plop her inside.
He closes the front door.

INT. JOHN'S NEW HOUSE - NIGHT

Emily stands in one place and looks around the empty house.

                    JOHN
        You said you were going to come
        over at noon so I figured you
        weren't coming at all.

                    EMILY
          Yeah, I was with Whitney. I bought
          a gun so I could go to the
          shooting range with her.

                    JOHN
          You have a gun? Abe let you get a
          gun? You've been suicidal before,
          that's not a good idea! How could
          he let you do that?

                    EMILY
          He encouraged it! He wants people
          to do everything and anything that
          will make them happy. Even if it's
          killing them self, but that's not
          why I have a gun, thanks.

                    JOHN
          Stop defending him and those
          people. They're crazy!

Emily gets defensive.

                    EMILY
          Well, Abe asked me not to see you
          anymore. I think he was right
          about you the whole time.

                    JOHN
          What? What are you saying? He's
          just brainwashing you, I wish
          you'd realize that!

                    EMILY
          You know what, John? I don't care!
          I feel better than ever. I came
          over to see if I could be happy
          with both, but I know I can't be.

Emily turns around to open the front door. John pushes
against the door so she can't leave.

                    JOHN
          What do you mean both? You mean be
          a part of that group and be with
          me?

                    EMILY
          I did, but now I see Abe was
          right.

John swallows his pride and ignores the comment.

>   JOHN
>   Emily, I really like you and I'm
>   really trying to help...but the
>   relationship you have with Abe is
>   fucking weird and it pisses me off
>   so I wouldn't want both for you. I
>   know what you're thinking is
>   what's best, but it really isn't.
>   But I'm not going to try and
>   convince you. So if you'd rather
>   be in that group than with me,
>   then fine.

>   EMILY
>   ...Fine.

Emily opens the front door again. John rolls his eyes and
shakes his head. John follows Emily out the door.

EXT. JOHN'S NEW HOUSE - NIGHT

Emily is marching down the driveway to her car. John pulls
her by her arm.

>   JOHN
>   Emily, think about what you're
>   doing.

Emily pulls her arm from John and slaps him across his
face.

>   EMILY
>   Don't ever grab me like that
>   again!

>   JOHN
>   Jesus Christ, I didn't even hurt
>   you, you're just walking away when
>   you should be working this out
>   with me!

>   EMILY
>   Don't talk to me like that. You
>   never wanted to help me, you just
>   wanted to help yourself.

John follows Emily to her car.

>   JOHN
>   Emily, if I really didn't care
>   about you, I wouldn't be telling
>   you to stay away from those
>   people.

Emily is at her car and she pushes John away from her.

                    EMILY
          And they're telling me to stay
          away from you!

                    JOHN
          Emily, don't be stupid just
          because more people are telling
          you what's right! Just come back
          to reality. I could sense
          something weird with everyone
          there which is why I left and this
          just proves how right I was!

Emily grunts and rolls her eyes.

                    EMILY
          I really don't want to see you
          ever again.

Emily gets in her car and slams the door. John is
frustrated and has his hands on the back of his head.

                    JOHN
          Why are you being so immature?

Emily speeds away and he watches her leave in amazement.

                    JOHN (CONT'D)
          Un-fucking-believable.

John is still angry but walks back into his house.

INT. COFFEE SHOP - DAY

Emily and Erin sit in a coffee shop. Emily drinks an iced
coffee while Erin has a hot drink.

                    ERIN
          A cult? Our help group isn't a
          cult! I can't believe you're even
          asking that. Obviously John is
          going to say that!

                    EMILY
          Look, you're the one I trust most
          and I'm trying to be really open
          and honest right now.

                    ERIN
          What makes you think it would be a
          cult? You think cults even still
          exist?

                    EMILY
          You've been there longer than I
          have. Do you think people just
          blindly follow or worship Abe?

                    ERIN
          What?

                    EMILY
          I've been trying to find out
          characteristics of cults but-

                    ERIN
          Are you in danger? No. So what's
          wrong with being happy? If you're
          happy with the help group, then
          you need to stay, whether it is a
          cult or not. You're a committed
          member now, you can't ruin this
          for everyone else.

                    EMILY
          Yeah...I just realize how time-
          consuming this cult, I mean, help
          group is and then I think about
          John because Abe asked me not to
          see him anymore.

                    ERIN
          Well of course. Abe knows what
          he's talking about. He knows
          what's best for us, he's just
          trying to protect you.

                    EMILY
          I just don't think I want to do
          this anymore. I should be able to
          come in and out of meetings like a
          normal help group like John was
          saying.

Emily gets up from her seat.

                    ERIN
          Where are you going?

                    EMILY
          I just need to think.

Emily starts to head out of the coffee shop.

                    ERIN
               (shouting to Emily)
          Will I see you on Tuesday?

                        EMILY
              I don't know.

Erin gets out her phone and calls Abe.

                        ERIN
              Abe, I think we have a Lauren
              problem.

INTERCUT:

EXT. LAUREN'S HOUSE - DAY

Lauren is lifeless on her bed with a hole in her skull.

There is a black pistol in her hand. There are sirens in
the background. Her cellphone is on the bed too.

Abe has his phone pinched between his ear and shoulder, and
he cleans his silver gun of blood with a rag.

                        ABE
              What do you mean? I just fixed the
              Lauren problem?

                        ERIN
              You know like Tyler and
              Marie...but with Emily.

                        ABE
              Oh. We have a lost member...Sad,
              she just became official at our
              fundraiser last weekend. Thanks
              for telling me, we'll have to do
              something quick before she doesn't
              need us anymore. I'll see how I
              can help.

EXT. MARIGOLD CHURCH PARKING LOT - DAY

Emily sits in her car and cries. Abe knocks on the window.
She wipes her tears away quickly and gets out of her car.

                        EMILY
              Abe! Hi.

                        ABE
              I noticed something was up, tell
              me what's on your mind.

Emily comes up with an answer quick to satisfy Abe.

                    EMILY
          I'm just upset because I really
          want to apologize to John but I
          know you say he's bad for me.

                    ABE
          That's right, just look at how
          he's making you feel right now. I
          see how jumbled you've been
          lately. If you listen to me and
          let him go, it will make you feel
          better for the future. However, if
          you keep trying to contact him,
          you're breaking my trust.

Emily's head hangs low.

                    EMILY
          Yeah. I understand.

                    ABE
          But tell me what you do.

Abe puts his hand on her shoulder and walks back into the
church. Emily gets back in her car and starts it.

INT. MARIGOLD CHURCH - DAY

There are twenty members still huddled in the center of the
church. Abe walks in the room and they turn their attention
to him.

                    ABE
          You all know recently how I was
          finally able to take care of
          Lauren after she left us.
          Unfortunately, we already have
          another person that's abandoning
          us and with her boyfriend putting
          things in her head, it could harm
          us later.

                    ROB
          It's Emily, isn't it?

Rob is upset, he shakes his head.

                    ABE
          It is, Rob.

The members gasp.

                    ABE (CONT'D)
          I know, it's a shame after
          everything, not just I have done,
          but you have done for her as well.
          We're going to move forward as if
          she's an ex-member.

Abe walks through the crowd and they move over for him. He
sits down in a chair while everyone else stands.

                    ABE (CONT'D)
          So this is what we're going to do,
          I have a feeling she's going to
          call John today, meaning she made
          her decision about how she feels
          for us.

INT. ACE MARKETING FIRM - DAY

John is in the middle of a meeting, sitting at the head
chair while a CLIENT (30) sits at the other end of the
table. FOUR MEN and ONE WOMAN fill the chairs.

                    CLIENT
          I'm begging for your guys' help
          here, my dad's company has been
          going downhill and I think it's
          because he's not changing
          anything. His website hasn't even
          been updated since it was
          invented...

Everyone shares a small laugh.

The client talks while John's phone vibrates in his bag
next to him. He doesn't even look at his phone to see who
it is, he just mutes it.

INT. EMILY'S APARTMENT - DAY

Emily lays on her couch and tears stream down her face.
Paul rubs against her. Her phone is to her ear.

                    EMILY
          I know you're at work and can't
          even talk to me right now, but I'm
          sorry. I always wanted to be with
          you, I just wanted friends and
          people who actually cared about
          me. I thought it was the group
          making me happy but it was just
          you. Please call me as soon as you
          can, John.

INT. MARIGOLD CHURCH - DAY

Abe continues with his preaching.

                    ABE
          We can't play around like we did
          with the others. In fact, we'll
          have to do it faster than we did
          with Lauren or Marie.

Abe looks at MARK (29) who's wearing a button down.

                    ABE (CONT'D)
          Mark, since you're dressed to
          impress, I'll need you to help me
          with something.

INT. ACE MARKETING FIRM - NIGHT

John leaves his office. He listens to Emily's voicemail and
he has a sad smile.

Mark is there, he watches John from a short distance. John
sees Mark but doesn't acknowledge him as a threat.

John turns his back to Mark and calls Emily. Mark doesn't
let the first ring go through; he rips the phone out of
John's hands and throws it across the room into the
concrete wall. Mark sprints out of the building.

                    JOHN
                (bewildered)
          Whu...why the fuck would you do
          that? Who are you?

John walks to his phone and an EMPLOYEE (female, 25) picks
it up for him.

                    EMPLOYEE
          What was that about?

                    JOHN
          I don't fucking know, I'm just as
          confused as you are!

The phone's screen is so cracked that the phone can't turn
on. John sighs with anger and disbelief.

                    JOHN (CONT'D)
          Does he even work here? He needs
          to be fired!

INT. ABE'S HOUSE, BEDROOM - NIGHT

Abe stands in front of his closet with just jeans on. His
chest and stomach have a few odd scars and the rest is
covered in hair.

Abe compares two Hawaiian shirts on hangers, one is red and
the other is blue. Whitney comes up from behind him and
hugs him.

                    WHITNEY
          You are such a great leader. Do
          you think you'll take care of
          Emily tonight?

                    ABE
          Oh yeah. It'll be hard though,
          getting her to do it. She hasn't
          been in long enough to instantly
          do what I say, especially because
          of that John guy.

                    WHITNEY
          You'll do great, sweetie. You
          always do.

Whitney kisses his cheek.

                    WHITNEY (CONT'D)
          Save some blood for me.

She laughs and walks away.

                    WHITNEY (O.S.)
          And go with the red one, that's
          your lucky shirt.

INT. EMILY'S APARTMENT - NIGHT

She lays on her couch and Paul comes by. She cries.

                    EMILY
          I feel awful, Paul. Damn, I suck.

Emily calls John's cellphone but it goes straight to
voicemail. Emily assumes it's because he doesn't want to
talk to her.

                    EMILY (CONT'D)
          John, please don't ignore me. I
          know I am being weird but it's
          only because I really wanted a
          place but now I'm rethinking
          everything. I just want you to
          know I'm sorry. Please don't
          ignore me.

She hangs up.

                    EMILY (CONT'D)
               (crying)
          I deserve this.

INT. PHONE STORE - NIGHT

John talks to the SALESMAN at the phone store.

                    SALESMAN
          Would you like to buy a tablet
          with your new phone? We can
          upgrade your plan.

                    JOHN
          No thanks. I literally just asked
          for the same phone and the same
          number.

                    SALESMAN
          Are you sure? Because if you
          upgrade now, you can put three
          more people on your plan for the
          price of two.

                    JOHN
          I don't need other people on my
          phone plan, I just need my phone
          replaced with the same phone
          number...

INT. EMILY'S APARTMENT - NIGHT

Emily sits up on her couch.

                    EMILY
          John, I'm calling your house
          because I don't know what else to
          do, please don't be mad at me.
          Please don't think that I was
          picking Abe over you.
               (MORE)

                    EMILY (CONT'D)
          I don't want to do this anymore, I
          don't want to do anything. I'm so
          sorry.
                    (crying)
          I feel like I've lost everything
          and that all my progress is going
          to be ruined...

Emily slams her phone down and covers her hand over her wet
eyes.

EXT. EMILY'S APARTMENT BUILDING - NIGHT

Abe waits at the front door of the apartment building.

CARRIE (20) opens the door from the inside.

                    CARRIE
          Hi, Abe.

                    ABE
          How's it going, Carrie? Thanks for
          letting me in.

                    CARRIE
          No problem! Glad I could help.

                    ABE
          Now go back up to your room. I'll
          see you on Monday for the next
          meeting.

INT. EMILY'S APARTMENT FRONT DOOR - NIGHT

Abe knocks gently on Emily's door.

INT. EMILY'S LIVING ROOM - NIGHT

Emily sits up from hearing the knocking. She's completely
bewildered at who it could be.

                    EMILY
          Hello? Who is it?

She sniffles and wipes away tears.

                    ABE (O.S)
          It's Abe. Just wanted to check on
          you is all.

Emily walks to the door with a small grin.

She opens the door.

>   EMILY
> That's so sweet of you to check on
> me, but I'm fine, Abe.

>   ABE
> Is John here, did you ever call
> him?

>   EMILY
> I did but, no answer.

Abe grins and chuckles to himself.

Abe pushes Emily inside and brings himself in. He shuts and locks the door behind him.

INT. JOHN'S HOUSE - NIGHT

John places a bag with his new phone inside on the table.

He plugs his new phone in that's completely dead.

He hears the message machine beeping. He plays Emily's message to him.

>   EMILY FROM MESSAGE MACHINE
>   John...

INT. EMILY'S APARTMENT, LIVING ROOM - NIGHT

Abe moves away from the door. He grabs Emily by the hair and takes her phone off of the table. He drags her to the bedroom.

>   EMILY
>   (screaming)
> Let go! What are you doing?

>   ABE
> The fact that you called John is
> proof that I come second to you.
> You're not a real member.

INT. EMILY'S APARTMENT, BEDROOM - NIGHT

Emily is on her knees, down by Abe's feet. He still has her by the hair and looks through her closet. She's scared and starts to cry.

                    EMILY
          Wait! Give me another chance! I
          didn't know this is what you
          meant!

                    ABE
          Is this what you want to die in?
          Or would you like to put on
          something nicer?

Emily cries harder. Abe throws Emily on the bed.

                    ABE (CONT'D)
          Don't move. Where's your gun at?

Emily silently cries. He points his silver .40 S&W revolver
at her.

                    ABE (CONT'D)
          Where's your gun at? I know you
          it's here, I have Whitney make
          every new member get one. So,
          where is it?

                    EMILY
          It's in the closet. Floor. What
          are you going to do?

Abe finds the gun case under clothes and pulls her .380
out.

                    ABE
          Are you happy with leaving?

Abe puts the .380 in his pocket. He pulls the hammer back
on his revolver. Abe places the revolver in Emily's hands
and makes the gunpoint up under her chin.

                    EMILY
          What do you mean? I didn't leave!
          I want to be in your group!

                    ABE
              (calmly)
          That's not what your actions are
          saying. But don't worry, this is
          just how all members leave. I'm
          gonna need you to kill yourself.

Emily starts crying again.

                    EMILY
          I can't.

ABE
          Emily, that's just fear talking
          and for once, I want you to make
          me happy and not think about
          yourself.

                    EMILY
          I don't think I want to do this,
          though.

                    ABE
          You proved to me desperately that
          you do. If you want to make me
          happy you will.
                    (beat)
          Plus, your three months are up,
          and you're still not who you want
          to be. You're still not happy.

Emily thinks for a second.

                    EMILY
          But, I don't want to die right
          now. I can't.

                    ABE
          Yes, you can. It's the only way,
          Emily. What's the difference if
          it's now or months ago when you
          really wanted to do it?

                    EMILY
          No, John was right. I shouldn't
          kill myself and you shouldn't be
          trying to help me in that way.

Abe sees he can't talk Emily into doing what he wants like
everyone else. He changes his tactics. He stands up
straight.

                    ABE
          Then do it for John. Pull that
          trigger and show John he was right
          all along but so wrong for not
          being there for you.

Emily hesitates.

                    ABE (CONT'D)
          You said you tried calling him.

She doesn't respond. Abe's yell spooks her.

>   ABE (CONT'D)
> You did! He wasn't there. I was
> right. He won't ever be there for
> you. You should make him feel bad
> for abandoning you. Make him feel
> guilty. Make him miss you so he
> knows how it feels.

Emily's mind races.

>   ABE (CONT'D)
> If you're not going to do it for
> me, do it for John. He'd want
> this.

>   EMILY
> No! I don't care what either of
> you want! Because I don't want
> this!

Abe is speechless but angry. He's never had someone think
so independently before.

>   ABE
> Then why are you still holding
> that gun under your chin? It's
> because you know it's what you
> should do finally!

>   EMILY
> No! It's not!

She starts crying harder.

>   EMILY (CONT'D)
> It's because I don't know what
> you're going to do to me if I
> don't keep it here...

Abe pauses. His head lifts up, his confidence is back
because he still holds power over her.

>   ABE
> Damn right.

Abe pulls out his phone.

>   ABE (CONT'D)
> Now I'm going to have you call
> someone. You're going to tell them
> you are going to kill yourself
> right now.

Emily nods her head yes with the barrel of the gun under
her chin.

                    EMILY
                (crying)
        Okay...

Abe dials the suicide hot-line off of Emily's phone. He
hands her the phone while it rings.

                    EMILY (CONT'D)
        Who are you calling?

                    ABE
        Suicide hotline. It makes it more
        convincing to the police when
        you're always using two different
        bullets.

Emily puts the phone to her ear.

                    ABE (CONT'D)
                (smiling)
        You're on hold, aren't you?

Abe laughs.

AMY from the suicide hotline answers. Emily has it on
speaker.

                    AMY
        Hello, this is the crisis
        helpline, I'm Amy.

                    EMILY
                (crying)
        Hi Amy. My name is Emily and... I
        am going to kill myself.

                    AMY
        Emily, please don't do that. You
        are worth everything. Talk to me
        for a bit so-

Abe rolls his hand for Emily to continue.

                    EMILY
        I just can't do it anymore. I'm
        sorry.

Emily hangs up and throws her phone down.

                    ABE
        Great. Thanks for helping me with
        this Emily. Are you happy you
        won't be hated by the Marigold
        members at least?

>   EMILY
>   Fuck you and Marigold.

Abe is mad she isn't interested in Marigold. He's used to
ex-members begging to come back in while on their death
bed.

>   ABE
>   Emily, you don't know what you
>   want because you're feeling numb.
>   You're always going to have this
>   feeling so you should just do it
>   already. You've tried everything.
>   You matter to no one. Not even
>   your boyfriend.

Emily thinks about what he's asking of her.

>   EMILY
>   I don't need to matter to John. I
>   matter to myself and Paul.

She laughs pitifully.

>   ABE
>   Oh, shut the fuck up with the
>   pathetic you-matter-to-yourself
>   shit.

Emily talks while the gun shakes in her hands. Abe pulls a
sheet of paper with print on it out of his pocket.

>   ABE (CONT'D)
>   Would you like to read the suicide
>   note I made for you?

Emily holds the gun with one hand and reaches out to read
the paper.

Her cell phone starts to ring. Close to her phone is her
Marigold list with all of her goals and a dried up marigold
flower.

>   EMILY
>   Is it John?

>   ABE
>   Hm, seems a little early for the
>   police to call you but maybe Amy
>   is good at her volunteer work.

Abe looks at her phone on the nightstand.

                    ABE (CONT'D)
          I recognize that number from
          anywhere. It's a different hotline
          calling. Did you call anyone else
          besides John?

                    EMILY
          No, just John. His cell phone and
          landline, I left a message.

                    ABE
               (to himself, mad)
          Seriously? Who the fuck still has
          a landline?

Abe rips the note out of Emily's hand and slams it next to
her nightstand on top of her list and crushes the dead
flower.

                    EMILY
          So he does care.

                    ABE
          No. Of course not. He called the
          police and the hotline so he can't
          feel guilty for your death. But I
          thought you didn't care about John
          anyway.

                    EMILY
          I'm just saying you were wrong.

Abe sits on the bed next to Emily and puts his arm around
her. She relaxes her hands but he picks them up so the gun
is placed back under her chin. He gazes at his revolver,
smiling because he's imagining the possibilities it holds.

                    ABE
          Emily, I'm not going to let you
          get out alive today, so let me
          tell you something I've seen many
          times. Suicide really is a
          beautiful thing. You won't have to
          worry about anything anymore.

INT. JOHN'S AUDI - NIGHT

John speeds to Emily's apartment but there's traffic.

John is stuck behind a car at a red light.

                    JOHN
          Fuck!

INT. EMILY'S APARTMENT, BEDROOM - NIGHT

Abe gets up from her bed and stands across from her.

                    ABE
          I can tell by your eyes how dead
          you're feeling. Trust your gut
          Emily, pull the trigger. Do the
          world this favor.

                    EMILY
          Were you there when it happened to
          Marie?

INT. MARIE'S HOUSE - NIGHT

Flashback to Abe at Marie's house, the same woman from the
first scene. She's lifeless on the bed. Abe takes his
silver revolver from her hand and places a .9mm there.

Then he heads out of the bedroom. As Abe walks out of the
back door, Cop 1 and Cop 2 bust through the front door and
run straight up to her room.

INT. EMILY'S APARTMENT, BEDROOM - NIGHT

Abe stares at Emily before answering.

                    ABE
          I like to say goodbye to all the
          ex-members.

                    EMILY
          Please don't make me do this. I'll
          come back to Marigold, I'll stay
          away from John. Just please, don't
          kill me or make me kill myself.

                    ABE
          Sorry, you lost my trust. And I
          don't want you back in my group.

EXT. EMILY'S APARTMENT BUILDING - NIGHT

John runs out of his car to the front of the apartment. He
speaks through the intercom.

                    JOHN
          Emily. Let me up! I don't have a
          key for this place anymore.

John waits for a response but there's nothing. He kicks the door once but it doesn't break.

INT. EMILY'S APARTMENT, BEDROOM - NIGHT

Emily perks her head up. Abe's eyes widen and he gets angry. Abe takes Emily's .380 out of his pocket.

                    ABE
          Don't get up.

Emily takes the gun and points it at Abe. She's shaking.

She's scared but has some confidence now that someone is here for her.

                    ABE (CONT'D)
               (like a mother
               disciplining her
               annoying kid)
          Don't point that at me.

Emily puts the gun back to her. The confidence is gone.

EXT. EMILY'S APARTMENT BUILDING - NIGHT

John pushes the other intercom buttons.

                    JOHN
          Carter, are you there? It's John,
          can you just let me in real quick?
          I need to get up to my old
          apartment.

CARTER'S VOICE (50) comes on over the intercom.

                    CARTER'S VOICE
          Sure, here you go.

                    JOHN
          Thanks, thank you!

The door buzzes and John rushes inside.

INT. EMILY'S APARTMENT, BEDROOM - NIGHT

Abe relaxes against the dresser.

                    ABE
          I'll make a deal with you Emily,
          something I've never done before.
                    (MORE)

                              ABE (CONT'D)
                    You're going to shoot John and
                    I'll let you live. The other
                    option is that I kill you both
                    before you can even point my
                    revolver away from you.

                              EMILY
                    No, I can't.

                              ABE
                    If you don't want to kill John,
                    you can just let him live and kill
                    yourself. I promise I won't hurt
                    him.

Abe smiles.

                              EMILY
                    No! I'm not going to do either!

She sets the gun down.

                              ABE
                    I know you can't pull the trigger
                    on anyone but God help me, put
                    that barrel back under your chin
                    or else you and John have no
                    chance.

She puts the revolver back under her chin like Abe demands.

Emily and Abe hear John pound and yell at her door.

                              JOHN (O.S)
                    Emily! Let me in! Now!

                              EMILY
                    John! I'm in here! Abe's here too!

Emily watches Abe cock the .380. Her eyes get wide.

EXT. EMILY'S APARTMENT DOOR - NIGHT

John realizes what it means to have Abe inside her
apartment. He starts to kick her front door. On the third
kick, it busts the door open.

There's a gunshot.

John pauses in shock.

INT. EMILY'S APARTMENT, BEDROOM - NIGHT

Abe leans relaxed on her dresser he has blood splatter on
his face. Emily's blood splatter is everywhere and she's
lifeless on her bed. John runs in. John collapses to his
knees from the shock.

                    JOHN
              (tearing up, whispering)
          No.

Abe still leans on the dresser and talks down to John.

                    ABE
              (laughing, smiling)
          Ope! Someone was too late! You
          just missed it!

Abe walks to Emily's body. He pulls a .380 casing out of
his pocket and takes a bullet out of .380's chamber.

                    JOHN
          Why would you do this.
              (beat)
          I called the cops, they're on the
          way. You're not going to get away
          with this.

                    ABE
          Are you just talking to make
          yourself feel better? I wouldn't
          be too upset, she chose you.

                    JOHN
          What?

Abe puts the .380 casing where the .40 casing lays.

                    ABE
          Want to know why I always make
          them use my forty instead of the
          gun I get them to buy when they
          join?

John looks up at Abe and starts to rise on his feet.

                    ABE (CONT'D)
          It's the splatter.

Abe wipes Emily's blood that got on his cheek with his
thumb. Then he licks it.

He takes his silver revolver from her hands and replaces it
with the .380. Abe wipes the revolver off with the bottom
of his Hawaiian shirt.

                    JOHN
          What the fuck is wrong with you,
          you can't possibly think you're
          getting away with this.

                    ABE
          Of course I can. I've done this
          twelve times in the past four
          years. It's been a busy year. It's
          just a simple suicide to the cops.
          Makes sense with all the mental
          illness happening today. Usually,
          I wait until they're in for a
          year, or are threatening our
          secret before I make them face
          this kind of consequence. But
          goddamn, I get really excited when
          anyone wants to leave now. I just
          really love watching them pull the
          trigger.
                    (laughing)
          Anyway...

Abe puts one more bullet in his revolver. John's anger
grows, he grinds his teeth and tightens his fists.

                    ABE (CONT'D)
          I've never staged a double suicide
          before.

John tackles Abe into the wall before he can finish loading
the gun. Abe hooks John in the stomach. John punches Abe
across his face and starts tackling him again, this time,
John takes Abe out the second story bedroom window with
him.

EXT. EMILY'S APARTMENT BUILDING - NIGHT

Two cop cars pull in front of the building and see the two
men fall out of the building together.

OFFICER FREEMAN (30, Caucasian) and OFFICER ALBU (40,
Caucasian) in one car watch the two of them fall.

                    OFFICER FREEMAN
          Holy fucking shit!

                    OFFICER ALBU
          Oh my god!

The two get out of the patrol car. They talk to the other
TWO OFFICERS while they sit in their car.

                    OFFICER FREEMAN
              We're going to call an ambulance
              for these two, get to room
              two-zero-nine.

EXT. EMILY'S APARTMENT BUILDING - NIGHT

Abe and John lose their breath and can barely move. John
crawls to Abe. John punches him once but it's not that hard
from how hurt they are.

Abe blocks a punch and hits John back. John punches Abe
again. Both of them are bleeding on their faces from the
window and the fall.

Officer Freeman and Officer Albu run next to them and
Freeman pulls John away from Abe.

John accidentally elbows Freeman.

John punches Abe one last time before the cops tackle John
and put him in handcuffs.

INT. HOSPITAL ROOM - DAY

John lies in a hospital bed in a gown. He has bruises and
cuts all over him. A NURSE helps John sit up on his
hospital bed. John has a dead, monotone look on him.

                    NURSE
              How's your back feeling?

                    JOHN
              I can't really feel anything.

                    NURSE
              That means the morphine's working.

                    ABE (O.S)
              Knock, knock.

                    NURSE
              Oh, looks like you have a visitor,
              I'll be back.

Abe swipes the private curtain. He's in an arm sling and
has flowers. Abe has bruises and cuts on his face too.

                    ABE
                 (mocking)
              How ya feeling? These are for you.

Abe hands John the flowers but he doesn't take them. Abe tosses the flowers in the trash.

                    JOHN
          Why the fuck are you here?

                    ABE
          I'm just here to remind you that
          you can't win. I know everyone and
          enough members are involved with
          the justice system. And to the
          others who aren't, they don't care
          to investigate. As I said, it's
          another simple suicide to them.

                    JOHN
          Why didn't she just shoot you? I
          don't get it.

                    ABE
          I was her God. She couldn't kill
          me. People go their whole lives
          and the only person they kill are
          themselves.

                    JOHN
          I don't care what you say I'm not
          going to let you get away with
          this.

                    ABE
          Look, I don't have time for
          another court case, I'm trying to
          go national here. You're not going
          to win. You're serving time for
          hitting that cop.

John thinks about what Abe tells him. John rests back in the hospital bed

                    JOHN
          Alright. Fine. If I don't take you
          to court for this can you get me
          out for hitting the cop?

Abe ponders on it for a second.

                    ABE
          I don't know, I fucking hate you.
          But it was really fun watching
          Emily take her life. She was
          different everyone else. It was
          nice to have a little change.

John chokes up from hearing about his girlfriend's last
moments but sucks it up in front of Abe.

                    ABE (CONT'D)
          You want me to explain it to you?

                    JOHN
          Fuck you.

                    ABE
          Okay, the deal is, I'll give you a
          get out of jail free card since
          Whitney is the judge, but only if
          you let me tell you.

John clenches his jaw and Abe smiles. Abe sits on the edge
of John's bed.

                    ABE (CONT'D)
          I told Emily, it was her or you. I
          said I was going to kill you if
          she didn't kill herself.
                    (beat)
          She did it for you. You're the
          reason she's dead.

A tear runs down John's face, he tries to hold his anger
and sadness back but can't.

                    ABE (CONT'D)
          You guys have only been dating for
          a few months, I can't believe
          she'd do that for you.

Abe pats John's shoulder.

                    ABE (CONT'D)
                    (laughing)
          You had yourself a keeper. I'll
          see you on the other side. Glad we
          could make this deal.

Abe leaves John's hospital room and shuts the curtain
behind him.

EXT. GRAVEYARD - DAY

John walks to Emily's grave alone. He places flowers on her
grave.

                    JOHN
          Why would you shoot yourself for
          me? God.
                    (MORE)

                    JOHN (CONT'D)
          This didn't have to happen.
               (beat)
          It's okay, I'm doing what I can to
          bring him and the entire cult
          down.

INT. PRIVATE INVESTIGATOR'S OFFICE - DAY

A private investigator, LIZ HANNON (female, 36) and a
lawyer, DENNIS MULLEN (male, 45) sit down together in her
office. The two shake hands.

                    DENNIS
          Hi, Dennis Mullen. Private
          attorney.

                    LIZ
          I'm Elizabeth Hannon, private
          investigator, but call me Liz.
          Thanks for coming in.

                    DENNIS
          Of course, it's about time we meet
          in person. I think it's a great
          idea that you work on the inside,
          but are you sure can handle it?
          Our client said it's a pretty
          serious cult. And I heard about
          what the leader has done to
          people.

                    LIZ
          Don't worry about me. After
          hearing what he told me, I think
          we have a solid case, we just need
          the proof. If half the world is on
          this leader's side, we need enough
          evidence that biased people
          couldn't deny.

                    DENNIS
          I can agree with that. Did he let
          you meet him?

                    LIZ
          No. He wants to keep himself out
          of it. Did he give you his name?

                    DENNIS
          No, he asked me to stay anonymous
          too. He's asking a lot.

LIZ
But for a good purpose.

INTERCUT:

INT. MARIGOLD BASEMENT - DAY

Abe speaks to a large group of people that watch him lead.

INT. PRIVATE INVESTIGATOR'S OFFICE - DAY

Dennis and Liz continue.

DENNIS
Our client wrote everything out
that he knows and what Abe has
told him. Our best bet is going
with the wrong sized bullet
hole in the head.

LIZ
I plan on using a video wire. It
might take a while but I'm just
excited to be a part of taking
this cult down.

INT. MARIGOLD BASEMENT - DAY

Abe walks up the basement steps into the main church floor.

He greets TWO NEW MEMBERS.

INT. PRIVATE INVESTIGATOR'S OFFICE

Liz pulls out a file.

LIZ
I made a medical record for my new
self. I now have depression and
recommended myself to a help
group.

DENNIS
Is this just in case they ask for
proof?

LIZ
We need to make this seem as real as possible.

EXT. GRAVEYARD - DAY

John still stands above her grave. He starts to pull out
her Marigold list and a pen. Some of her blood splatter is
on it.

                    JOHN
          It kind of pisses me off that life
          just keeps going on...A lot of
          people showed up for your funeral
          so that was nice. I didn't bring
          Paul but he's watching TV at my
          house right now. Your mom's not
          that crazy like you said...Met
          your dad too, I'm surprised he
          came. He did care about you.

John crosses off "meet my dad", "Have someone actually love
me back" and "Help someone else be happy off her list".

                    JOHN (CONT'D)
          For some reason, the attorney
          doesn't want me throwing away your
          fucking list so I figured I'd
          cross some things off for you.

He puts a bouquet of flowers on her grave and the list in
his pocket.

                    JOHN (CONT'D)
          Wish things could be different...I
          just hope Hannon and Mullen can
          take care of this before I do it
          myself.

John walks away. In the distance, Whitney leans against a
tree and watches John.

John sees Whitney and flicks her off while he walks the
other way. She smiles and turns away from the tree.

CUT TO BLACK:

END